THIS IS A WORK OF FICTION.

ANY SIMILARITY BETWEEN REAL

PERSONS, PLACES, OR THINGS, AND THE

FICTICIOUS PERSONS, PLACES, OR

THINGS PORTRAYED HEREIN, IS

ENTIRELY COINCIDENTAL.

Published by John Regan, 2022
North Palm Beach, FL

To order book: Amazon.com

or

www.heavenwhogetsin.com

or

johnregan2100@gmail.com

ISBN: 978-0-578-83492-4

Have you ever wondered where you're going after you die? Most people have, and if you're like most people you want to go to Heaven. But will you go directly to Heaven or to The Waiting Room? See for yourself as you witness the outcome of 12 very different individuals in this lightening fast read. Surely you will identify with one or more as they make this fascinating journey into the future of us all. Filled with wisdom, inspiration and plenty of humor, this compelling message will awaken you to the reality of God's immense love specifically for you. After all, He has already told us that He doesn't want even one of us lost.

"This is a Gem of a book! Not the kind you can put down. I so enjoyed reading every page – and am anxious to be able to hand out copies to everyone. It's the sort of book that doesn't impose but gets you in an intimate way - pondering your heart and thoughts. And every story is so compelling. We all know someone who fits every character in the story. I have so many people in my own life I would buy this for."

Christina Castagnaro

"Are you ready to take a peek at what happens when you die? Read this book if you want a dose of reality. The bonus will be a convincing look as to how you should live your life now."
Jack Land PhD   Co-founder South County Mental Health Center, Delray Beach, Florida

"It is so easy to get wrapped up in our day-to-day routines, and lives, and not acknowledge the reality of an afterlife, hopefully in Heaven. The book's major impact on me was its focus on Heaven. The dialogue was suspenseful and engaging. Also, I loved the prayers at the end. The book has had a positive impact on me."

Eve Carr

"John brings to life the words and teachings of God through dynamic characters, compelling dialogue, and exciting plot twists. A riveting tale infused with solid Christian doctrine, this book serves for readers as a way to learn the extent and strength of God's love for us. An enlightening book, *Heaven* paints The Waiting Room as what it is: a gift from God **because** He loves us."

Mrs. Anne Kearns, M.Ed
Grade 4 Language Arts Teacher
Reading Certified K-12

"The Lord has told us that we must become like little children to be able to truly appreciate the things of God and to enter His Kingdom of Heaven. This thought-provoking and prayerful book helps to show us what the Lord really means by that statement."

Tom Sherry , Author of "A Destiny to Die For"

"I loved the book!! Got it yesterday and was done by 7 this morning!! I gave it to my niece to read. I'm anxious for Bill to read it too. Excellent".

Mel Hill

"Our main goal in life, or should be, is to join God in Heaven. Reading this book will help us achieve that goal."   Don Kazimir

"The most important highlight of the book is that God's Mercy is truly His greatest attribute and heals the wounds of our souls."   DW

"I finished the book in two days, it was great. It was very creative and vivid. I don't usually read religious fiction, but you make it interesting."
                                        Casandra

"Beautifully written with uplifting messages of God's love. This grabbed my attention to help battle my anxiety. "Perfect love drives out fear" was my favorite chapter because it shapes the reality of what is true and what is not. John Regan gave me hope by showing the truth of God and driving out fear. This book is about the truth and the love of God."
                                PBA Grad Student

This book is a gift and a powerful wake-up call to experience the power that forgiveness can have in our lives and ultimately lead us to Heaven.
                                Faith Psillas

To order book:

Amazon.com

or

www.heavenwhogetsin.com

or

johnregan2100@gmail.com

Volume discounts available

Heaven

Who gets in
and
Who must wait

John Regan

To all the faithful who have
labored in the vineyard
in the hope of saving souls.
Your efforts will never be forgotten.

1

Surprise!

Tommy leaned his bicycle against the tall oak tree as he stared in amazement at the sign that read, '3 Miles to Heaven'. He had never seen the sign before even though he had passed this way every day while riding home from school. The arrow on the sign pointed down a winding country lane which puzzled him even more than the sign.

"This road wasn't here yesterday," he thought as he watched a car driven by an elderly man pass by and proceed down the lane. Almost immediately the car disappeared around a turn. At ten years of age, Tommy didn't have much resistance for his youthful curiosity and he immediately responded by jumping on his bike and racing after the car. Once around the turn, he noticed there were many bends and turns ahead and to his surprise, the car was nowhere in sight. Rounding the next turn, he began to smile as he gazed at the beautiful green fields and flowers covering the endless rolling hills. Approaching yet another turn, he passed an arrow shaped sign that read "one way."

"Gee, I wonder what that means" he shouted as he raced around the turn and was confronted by another sign that read "Slow speed - Checkpoint ahead." Tommy stopped pedaling and coasted as he stared at the long straightway ahead with a gate at the end. There was at least a quarter mile of road between him and the gate and the closer he moved toward the checkpoint, the better he could see someone sitting at a desk by the side of the road. And, there, stopped at the gate, was the car he had been chasing. Pedaling slowly, he passed a large sign with red letters that said "Stop Ahead." With two hundred feet remaining, he decided to pull off the road and slowly walk his bike toward the checkpoint. Unsure of his right to be there, he decided to just look and listen and wait for an opportunity to ask questions.

A middle-aged woman sitting at the desk was looking at her computer screen as she spoke with the elderly man who was driving the car. In front of his car was a long red and white arm which prevented him from moving forward. He could see it was the type that moves up and down with the push of a button.

"Good afternoon sir. What brings you here today?"

"I'm on my way to heaven. I died this morning."

"Yes sir. Thank you for your answer sir. May I have your name?"

"Harvey"

"And how old are you today Harvey?"

"Ninety-three, in excellent health, and I'm proud to say I have outlived all of my friends."

"Would you say, Harvey, that during your life you were more of a proud person or a humble person?"

"I have always been a very humble person."

"How about honesty, Harvey?"

"Yup! I've always told the truth."

"Were you merciful and forgiving?"

"If someone deserved forgiveness, well yeah, then I forgave them. But if they didn't, then I could not in good conscience forgive them."

"You mention conscience Harvey; has your conscience ever bothered you?"

"Not at all, I always did the right thing."

"And the last question Harvey, are you a loving person?"

"Whenever I feel like being a loving person, then I am loving, but when I don't feel like being a loving person, then I am not. Hey, you can't love everyone."

"Well thank you for your answers Harvey. Before I send you to Checkpoint Two, what do you plan on doing with your car? You really can't bring it to Heaven!"

"Excuse me madam, you don't understand. See, this car represents who I am. It's a very expensive car, one which most people could never afford. When people see me in this car, they look up to me. I worked very hard in business during my life and I deserve the best. See this watch, solid gold. When people see this they give me respect. Wherever I go, I get respect. My car and I are both going to Heaven; period!"

"Thank you, Harvey. Have a nice day."

As the gate was raised Harvey drove down the lane on his way to Checkpoint Two. As soon as he rounded the turn, and was out of sight, a tremendous pile of stuff appeared across the street from the desk. Tommy looked in amazement as he gazed upon a mountain of cars, boats, planes, jewelry, mansions, money, anything that would be part of the world and all its vanities. Breathless, he looked toward the woman as she smiled and asked, "Who are you young man, and what are you doing here?"

2

Inspiring

Cynthia's husband pulled his mini-van directly next to the '3 Miles to Heaven' sign and pushed the button to open the side door. Once the handicapped platform began to emerge, Cynthia set the brake on her wheelchair as she was slowly lowered to the ground. They had been married forty-seven years and both were in their late sixties. Cynthia was a very humble person and was never attracted to physical things of value. She rarely wore jewelry and relied on her husband to drive her to and from work. She believed they needed only one car and preferred to give much of what she would have spent on a car to various charities. If she had purchased a car, it would have needed special hand controls because she was unable to use her legs since her skiing accident twenty years earlier. As she rolled her wheelchair onto the road, she turned to watch her husband return the platform to the van and close the door.

Slowly he approached her as he struggled to speak. "This is it Cynthia. This is the moment we never wanted to happen. I…"

Bob lost his voice as tears welled up in his eyes.

"Bob honey, don't worry, I'll be fine. We've prayed together for forty seven-years and God has always answered our prayers."

"Well, he didn't answer our prayers to cure you of cancer."

"Yes, I know, but He has His reasons, and His reasons are always for the good of our souls."

Cynthia reached up to hug Bob and he responded with his own hug and a kiss. She returned the kiss, then backed her wheelchair about twenty feet from Bob and slowly waved goodbye as tears streamed down her face. Spinning her chair around, she rolled to the first turn in the road and stopped. Overcome, she desperately needed just one last look at Bob. She turned to see him kneeling next to the van and praying. He didn't see her, but his prayer gave her the comfort she needed. Turning back, she rounded the first turn and was out of sight.

3

Many Questions

Tommy took a deep breath as he anxiously prepared to identify himself and explain his presence on the road to Heaven

"My name is Tommy and, well, you see I was riding home after school and I noticed this road which was never here before. Then a car drove past me so I decided to follow it. The sign said, '3 miles to Heaven,' but I think this is maybe only one mile."

"Yes, it is Tommy; exactly one mile. There are two more checkpoints. The next is one mile and the last is two more miles."

"What is this pile of stuff all about?"

"Those items represent all the false Gods people have in their hearts. They can't get into Heaven unless they worship God alone. Many worship stuff. They must love God with an undivided love."

"I thought we are supposed to love one another also."

"Yes, we are and when we do, we love God who created and dwells in others. You listened to me speaking with Harvey and you heard that he didn't want to leave his car. But he really didn't have his car. He was just putting his trust in the memory of his car, not in God. This pile of stuff is not real - it is just an illusion. But it represents what so many people have left behind in an effort to change and put their trust in God."

"Why wasn't it here when Harvey was here?"

"Because he might have made a decision to leave his car based on what he saw other people had done. It would not have represented a real change of heart. No one can see the pile until they leave something."

"Why do people worship stuff instead of God?"

"They want people to admire them and love them and they think that stuff will impress others and then they will be loved. But the secret to being loved is to give love. Then others will love you in return and you will love yourself."

"What will happen to Harvey if he doesn't give up his car?"

"He won't be able to get into Heaven. But he still has two more chances."

"May I follow him and see what he does?"

"If you assure me that you will follow whatever instructions the angel at Checkpoint Two gives you."

"I will."

"Go ahead."

As the gate was raised Tommy jumped on his bicycle and raced to catch Harvey. Rounding the first turn, his mind raced back to last week's lesson at Sunday school. His teacher had suggested that each student ask God to give them a special way in which to serve Him. It could be to volunteer at a charity, or helping older people with chores, or praying for others. The choice was theirs and next Sunday they could share their experiences with the class.

"Could this be it?" Tommy thought. "Could this be what God has for me to do even though I don't know what it is? I guess I'll just have to wait and see."

4

Almost Home

Cynthia rolled around the last turn and stared at the straightway that led to Checkpoint One.

"Wow, it looks like it's all downhill, I can just coast there and save my energy. "

As she began her descent, she noticed the woman sitting at the desk.

"Gee, I hope I don't need any identification, I left it at home," she said to herself.

A few minutes later, as she gradually applied the brakes to her wheelchair, the woman at the desk greeted her.

"Good morning, and welcome to Checkpoint One."

"Hello, my name is Cynthia. I died a few hours ago and I'm on my way to Heaven. Am I going in the right direction?"

"Yes, you are Cynthia"

"Do I need any identification?"

"No, you don't Cynthia, but I do have a few questions."

"Sure, go ahead."

"How old are you?"

"I turned sixty-eight two months ago."

"Would you say you are a loving person?"

"I hope so. I certainly do try."

"How about being merciful and forgiving to others?"

"Uh...yes, I think so."

"Have you been an honest person during your life?"

"For the most part, although when I was younger I believe there were times when I was not completely honest."

"Do you have any questions?"

"Well, not really, this is all very new to me."

"Ok Cynthia, you are cleared to proceed to Checkpoint Two."

As the gate opened Cynthia turned her wheelchair and began rolling once again. As soon as she rounded the first turn, and was out sight, the immense pile of stuff appeared across the road.

"Too bad she didn't leave it" the angel whispered to herself. "She is such a nice person".

5

Major Decision

Harvey slowed his expensive automobile as he approached Checkpoint Two. Everything seemed the same except for the person at the desk. This time it was a middle-aged man who lowered the gate as Harvey came to a complete stop.

"Good morning Harvey, and welcome to Checkpoint Two."

"How did you know my name?"

"You're already in the system. I have you on my screen now."

"Ok, so what's next? I'm ready for Heaven."

"Harvey, I will ask you several questions as they appear on my screen. They are based on your responses at Checkpoint One and your life history."

"What is the purpose of the questions?"

"To help you get into Heaven."

"Fire away, I'm ready."

"Why do you insist on keeping your car, you can't bring it into Heaven?"

"It's who I am. It represents my status in society and gives me prestige and self esteem. I'm proud of my achievements."

"You were asked at Checkpoint One if you were a humble person and you said yes. Now you say you are proud. Which is it?"

"Hey, if you grew up the way I did you'd be the same way."

"What way?"

"Proud of your accomplishments; my father was always criticizing me and telling me I would never amount to anything. But I founded my own company and made a lot of money. I worked very hard at becoming somebody. Money, cars, and prestige prove that my father was wrong."

"Do you hold a grudge against your father?

"I don't hold grudges."

"Have you forgiven him?"

"I don't know."

"Why don't you know?"

"I don't know because I never thought about it."

"What did your father think about your success?"

"He died many years ago and I never asked him. We really didn't talk much."

"Well Harvey, you're not alive anymore and there is no one to impress. So why don't you leave your car here? Surely the people in Heaven don't care about your wealth or prestige or your car. They only care about you."

"If I leave my car here, do I go right into Heaven?"

"You still have one more checkpoint to go through and a few more questions. But whatever happens there, you still won't be allowed to bring your car into Heaven."

"Ok, Ok, I'll leave it. I really don't care about it anymore anyway. Open the gate, I'm ready."

Harvey jumped back in fright as a huge pile of stuff suddenly appeared across the street. He gasped as he saw his car at the very top with a large sign attached which read PRIDE in bold letters.

"You did it Harvey; you gave up your pride. Proceed to Checkpoint Three."

The gate opened and Harvey took off running just as Tommy rounded the turn and coasted to the gate.

"Oh bummer, I wanted to listen to Harvey."

"Who are you, little boy?"

"I'm Tommy, and I'm supposed to follow the instructions that the angel at Checkpoint Two gives me. But I don't see any angels."

"I'm an angel. How may I help you?"

"You're an angel? You don't look like an angel."

"What are angels supposed to look like?"

"You're supposed to have wings."

"We don't have wings. How may I help you?"

"I wanted to see if Harvey left his car; but when I came around the turn, I saw Harvey running to Checkpoint Three. Then I saw the pile of stuff but I didn't look to see if his car was in it. Now the pile is gone."

"One moment and I will re-display it for you."

"Oh wow! Awesome, he left it. What does that sign on top of it mean?"

"It means that in addition to his car, which was his false God, Harvey has also given up his pride."

"Will he go to Heaven now?"

"It depends on his answers at Checkpoint Three."

"Is it ok to follow him?"

"Will you follow the instructions of the angel at Checkpoint Three?"

"I will."

"Go for it."

6

Incorrigible

The angel at Checkpoint One spun her computer around and aimed the camera at a new arrival coming down the road. Pushing her intercom, she yelled; "Hey, Number Two, get a load of this." Laughing in amazement she stared at the teenage boy coming down the road on a Pogo stick.

"What's that?" Number Two shot back.

"That's a kid on a Pogo stick."

"I don't believe it."

"Believe it; he's almost here."

"Boing, Boing, bibbity bop bip, I'm cruisin' along on my very last trip, boing, boing" the boy sang as he bounced right over the gate and continued on his way to Checkpoint Two. Around the first turn he bounced past Cynthia, "Wahoo...Keep on wheelin' Freda, Boing, Boing, Boing."

"Hey, Number Two, he's heading your way. He didn't even stop. He bounced his way right over the gate. He's a real nut case."

"I see him; he's coming around the turn. Stop-Stop- you have to stop and go back to Checkpoint One."

"No way Jose, I'm on my way to Heaven."

The boy bounced his Pogo stick around in a big circle and with one super bounce landed right on top of the angel's desk.

"Boing, Boing, bibbity bop bip, I'm cruisin' along on my very last trip, Boing, Boing" he continued as he bounced his way toward checkpoint number three.

"Number Three, this is Number Two, the Pogo kid is on his way to you. I couldn't stop him."

Approaching the last turn, the Pogo kid passed Tommy and once he rounded the turn, he passed Harvey and, with a smile, yelled "Get a horse dude, ha ha."

"Number Three, this is Number One; absolutely send him back. He hasn't checked in yet. I don't even know who he is."

"No problem; he's almost here, I'll turn him around" the elderly man replied.

"Hey, where's Heaven?"

"Don't worry about it young man. You can't go anywhere from here but back to Checkpoint One."

"Why not? - I'm on my way to Heaven, I'm dead."

"You have to answer some questions to proceed. Go back."

"Bummer, total bummer!" he moaned as he turned around and started his return.

"What's your name? I'll send it to Number One"

"Billy."

"What was your cause of death?"

"I OD'd", Billy shouted as he bounced his way back to Checkpoint One.

7

Straight Forward

Cynthia wheeled closer to the shoulder of the road to give Billy plenty of room to bounce his way past her as he returned to Checkpoint One. As soon as he passed, she wheeled the last one hundred feet to the gate at Checkpoint Two.

"Hello, my name is Cynthia and I'm on my way to Heaven."

"Welcome Cynthia. I will have a few questions for you."

"Ok"

"Are you a humble person?"

"I hope so, but maybe I'm not perfectly humble."

"Would you consider yourself to be a charitable person?"

"When I was a youngster, there were times when I was not very charitable. But I'm much better now."

"Would your friends and family consider you to be holy?"

"Wow! I don't know the answer to that one."

"Thank you, Cynthia. You are cleared to proceed to Checkpoint Three."

8

Soul Searching

With every expectation of breezing right into Heaven, Harvey approached Checkpoint Three with a smile.

"Ok, I'm here. I know you have a few questions for me, but make it quick, I'm ready for Heaven."

"Welcome Harvey. It is my duty to inform you that depending on your answers, you will go either directly into Heaven, or, to the waiting room."

"Waiting room; what's that?"

"That is where you would go to establish the necessary change of heart in order to become like all those who are already in Heaven. You would, over time, develop the same virtues that they have."

"What virtues are you talking about?"

"There are many Harvey, the main ones would be, love, mercy, forgiveness, humility, charity, kindness, self-control, empathy, etc."

"Well, I have all of those I'm pretty sure."

"Do you hold any grudges against anyone?"

"No"

"Is there anyone whom you have not forgiven?"

"Probably not."

"How about your father?"

"Some people you forgive because you know that they are sorry for having offended you. But the ones that aren't sorry, well...they don't deserve forgiveness."

"Do you deserve forgiveness when you have sinned?"

"Well yeah; of course."

"Even if you are not sorry?"

"I'm always sorry for my sins."

"Are you sorry for not forgiving your father?"

"Why should I be? He doesn't deserve it."

"Why doesn't he deserve it?"

"Because he probably isn't sorry."

"How do you know he isn't sorry?"

"I don't really know because we never talked much. I just assume he isn't sorry."

"Well, he is dead now and you can't speak with him anymore, so the only thing left to do is forgive him. That will free up your conscience."

"I'll have to think about it."

"Harvey I will open the gate to the waiting room for you."

Suddenly, on the other side of the street a gate opened and a path to the waiting room appeared.

"It's right around the first turn Harvey. Have a nice day."

9

Childlike

The church bus arrived at the '3 Miles to Heaven' sign and stopped. The door opened and the driver emerged carrying a large tricycle which he placed on the road in front of the bus.

"Ok Sister Mary Ann, you're all set," he announced as he offered his hand to help the elderly nun step safely off the bus.

"Thank you, Gerald."

"You're welcome Sister; we will certainly miss you."

"And I will miss all of you, Gerald. Remember we can have a wonderful reunion if you and everyone in the parish follow in the footsteps of Jesus."

"We will do our best, Sister."

Sister Mary Ann began to pedal her tricycle down the country lane to Heaven singing as she went. "Jesus loves me this I know, because the Bible tells me so -"

Sister Mary Ann had been a very popular teacher of the faith to the young people in her parish for almost fifty years. Most of the adults in the parish had been instructed by her as youngsters themselves and willingly kept her on the staff as the years went by. Now, in her eighties, she was considering retirement when she suddenly contracted pneumonia and passed away. A holy soul, by any standard, many in the church regarded her as a saint. Rounding the second turn, she was now in view of the first checkpoint and was spotted by the angel at the desk.

"Guess what Number Two; we have another one of a kind coming down the road. It looks like a nun on a tricycle."

"Say again"

"I said a nun is riding a tricycle down the road to Heaven."

"Keep me posted as soon as you get some info, I have a feeling this will be a special case."

"Will do."

Even though he wasn't in on the conversation, the angel at Checkpoint Three heard it and also sensed that special circumstances were about to unfold.

Sister Mary Ann slowly pedaled to Checkpoint One and stopped at the gate.

"Welcome Sister. May I have your name?"

"Yes, I am Sister Mary Ann."

"Thank you, sister. I have a few Ques --- Oh! No, I do not have any questions Sister" the angel said with a look of surprise on her face. Her computer screen was completely filled with information on Sister Mary Ann and as she began to read it the gate automatically raised by itself.

"Ok Sister you are cleared to go to Checkpoint Two."

"Are you sure? Weren't you going to ask me some questions?"

"Well, we usually do ask questions Sister but in your case, you are already cleared to proceed."

"What kind of questions do you usually ask?"

"We ask people what kind of a life they have lived. If they are a loving person, a forgiving person, are they honest, generous or selfish, are they humble. And there are other questions from time to time."

"I must admit there were sometimes when I was not completely loving and forgiving, plus I do remember being selfish. And I'm embarrassed to say I was proud on more than one occasion."

"Thank you, Sister, for your honesty, but I do not have any questions for you. You are cleared to proceed to Checkpoint Two."

"Well, ok, I guess you know what you're doing. I'll just pedal down to the next checkpoint. Thank you for your assistance."

As Sister Mary Ann approached the first turn the angel whispered, "Hey, Number Two, she's on her way to you. My gate went up by itself."

"So did mine and my screen is completely filled with her info."

Just as Number One was about to inform Number Three, the pogo kid blasted around the turn and bounced right over Sister Mary Ann's head screaming, "Wahoo... Boing, Boing, bibbity bop bip, time to cancel my very last trip... Boing, Boing."

Number One tried to stop him, but he rushed right past her desk and headed back towards town.

"Hey...come back here...you're dead. You can't go back to town."

10

Disappointed

Tommy approached the last check point somewhat confused. "Hi, I'm Tommy and I was hoping to see Harvey as he went into Heaven, but I guess I'm too late."

"You just missed him Tommy, he didn't make it to Heaven, but he is in the waiting room."

"What is the waiting room?"

"It's the place where you spend the necessary amount of time to develop a change of heart. Harvey needed a change of heart."

"Why? He left his car and his pride back at number two."

"Tommy, you are aware of his car and pride because you saw the pile of stuff. That is what Harvey left behind. But he did not leave anything behind here and he was not permitted to proceed to Heaven because of it."

"What did he not leave behind?"

"His resentment and his unforgiveness towards his father. Do you remember the Lord's Prayer that Jesus taught his disciples? In it we find the words, 'Forgive us our trespasses as we forgive those who trespass against us.' Harvey did not want to forgive his father, and until he does, he won't be allowed into Heaven."

"How long do you think it will take him to forgive his father?"

"I have no idea, Tommy. That will be up to Harvey."

11

Turmoil

Billy's bouncing came to a surprising halt when he rounded the first turn on the road to Heaven and was staring at the road to town. Suddenly his pogo stick would no longer bounce, and his feet would no longer respond to his desire to walk. He turned to go back toward Heaven and his ability to walk was restored. But when he tried to walk toward the road to town, he could go no further.

"Oh wow! I want to go back home. I don't want to be dead. I should have listened to my counselor. I was clean for two months but then I wanted to party one more time with my friends; Mistake...big mistake!"

"Billy! Hey Billy, you have to come back and check in. You can't be on the road. No one else can pass you. You'll be holding up everyone."

Billy looked down the road to Heaven and could see the angel from Checkpoint One about two hundred feet away calling to him.

"I'm not going to Heaven. I changed my mind. I'm going home."

"You can't, you're dead. You have nothing to say about it."

"I have plenty to say about it. I'm going home."

"Billy, there will be people waiting at the beginning of the road. They will know they can't pass you, so return to Checkpoint One."

"No!"

Suddenly a man in medical scrubs entered the road to Heaven and was approaching Billy. He appeared to be about fifty years of age and had a very somber look on his face.

"Hey Dude! Why so sad?" Billy yelled.

"Who are you?" the man shot back.

"Name's Billy."

"Why are you just standing here Billy, this is the road to Heaven."

"I decided to go back home and get my life together, but for some reason my feet won't walk that way. I can only walk toward Heaven."

"You died before me and I can't pass you. So, start walking toward Heaven."

"Go around me. I'm not going to Heaven. They already sent me back to Checkpoint One to check in. And that is not on my agenda. I am, however, going to check out as soon as I figure out a way to make my feet work."

As they continued to discuss the dilemma, a woman arrived at the entrance to the road to Heaven and noticing that she could go no further, she sat down on a bench by the tree to wait. Immediately, another soul arrived at the entrance pulling a wagon full of bagels. He asked the woman sitting on the bench if he could proceed.

"No, you have to wait for me to go before you", she replied, "but I'm waiting for the doctor to move a little farther down the road so I can begin. Who are you?"

"My name is Milton Lumbagel. I'm a retired CPA."

"That's an unusual name. Why are you pulling a wagon full of bagels, Milton?"

"My wife Teresa died a number of years ago and I've been heartbroken ever since. She had very painful Lumbago for the last twenty years of her life. I couldn't help her with the pain, but because I knew how much she loved bagels, I would run to the bagel shop early in the morning and get her two fresh bagels. She liked most of the different types. Her favorite was the "everything" bagel; so, I would give her one of those in the morning to give her day a happy start. And then I would surprise her in the afternoon with one of the other types."

"Was your mother and father's last name Lumbagel?"

"No, their last name was Goldstein and so was mine until I changed it to Lumbagel. I missed Teresa so much I wanted to remember her in a positive light and my new last name accomplished that. I helped her by easing the pain of her Lumbago by distracting her with the happiness of her favorite bagels twice a day for twenty years. Now when I get to Heaven, I will be able to give her all the bagels she wants. I have fifty everything bagels and fifty assorted bagels in my wagon. I can't wait to see her. It has been twelve very lonely years since she died and -" Milton looked away as his voice began to weaken and tears gathered in his eyes.

"Milton, my name is Stephanie, and I'm a marriage and family counselor. Your love for your wife is music to my ears. I've spent most of my adult life trying to help married couples have a happy life together, but all too often love was the missing ingredient in so many of those marriages. I hope you will have a happy reunion with your wife."

"Thank you, Stephanie. I think we should finish this conversation in Heaven, but for now we better get going, I see more people heading our way."

As Stephanie started to walk down the road to Heaven, she could hear the doctor trying to convince Billy to turn around and begin moving toward Heaven.

"Billy you are making it difficult for everyone. Please start moving to the check point."

"Forget about it Doc. I'm staying put."

12

Conscience

Tommy had decided to remain at Checkpoint Three because he knew that Cynthia would soon be arriving.

"I know it's only a guess, but I really think that Cynthia will go directly to Heaven. She seems to be such a loving person."

Cynthia slowly approached Checkpoint Three with a look of reluctance on her face.

"Do I really have a right to go to Heaven? I don't feel worthy enough," she pondered as she wheeled toward the gate. The angel at the desk turned in Cynthia's direction and began typing information on his Keyboard. Each soul received an assessment written by the angel which indicated how much love filled the person's soul. Because of the prior two angels' assessments at Checkpoints One and Two, the third angel had a head start in determining what his assessment might be. By the time Cynthia arrived at the gate, he had already typed "a holy soul filled with love and kindness..." but he went no further than that without first interviewing her.

"Hello, my name is Cynthia," she uttered barely above a whisper.

"Welcome Cynthia. I have a few short questions for you." Cynthia nodded. "Do you love everyone, even your enemies?"

"Yes" Cynthia whispered.

"Do you hold any grudges against anyone?"

"No" she whispered once again.

"Do you love God?"

"Yes".

"Do you have any resentment towards God?"

Cynthia was silent.

The angel turned away from his computer screen and looked at Cynthia. "Do you hold anything against God?"

Cynthia had tears streaming down her face. She appeared to be struggling to speak but could not utter a sound. The angel was silent and sat back in his chair, giving Cynthia time to compose herself. Several minutes passed and Cynthia turned her wheelchair towards the angel and said, "I was always a strong defender of God to other people when they would make comments about my paralysis from my skiing accident. They would question the love and mercy of God and I always defended him. But then he allowed me to get cancer, which I suffered immensely from, and even then, I still defended Him. But when it came to the point that I had to leave my husband and children and all my friends whom I loved because it was time to die from my cancer, I just felt as though God had abandoned me. And now I don't know how I feel about Him. I'm sure I love Him, but I feel He has forgotten about me and now I resent Him. I want to be with Him in Heaven, but I don't want to approach Him with this resentment in my heart."

The angel responded with a very quiet voice looking directly into Cynthia's eyes. "I understand Cynthia. And God understands also. He loves you very much and wants you to be happy and will explain all of this to you when you are with Him. But for now, He wants you to be at peace as your love for Him grows once again. You can take all the time you need to forgive Him and to forgive yourself. When you are ready, He will welcome you with open arms." The angel stood and blessed Cynthia. The gate to the Waiting Room opened and Cynthia slowly wheeled down the path and through the door.

13

Reward

After watching Billy bounce his way back to Checkpoint One, and Cynthia entering the waiting room, Tommy didn't see anyone else approaching Checkpoint Three.

"Guess I'll just start pedaling back toward town to see if anyone else is on the way."

Rounding the last turn to Checkpoint Two, Tommy could see Sister Mary Ann approaching the gate which to his surprise was already open.

"Wow, the gate is open, and she hasn't even reached it yet."

Stopping behind the angel's desk Tommy listened to the conversation.

"Good afternoon Sister, welcome to Checkpoint Two. Usually, I have questions to ask, however, I have received word on my computer screen that you are cleared to Checkpoint Three. So, you are welcome to proceed."

"Well thank you, Checkpoint Two angel, but I must insist that you ask me some questions. I'm no better than the rest of the people on the road to Heaven."

"Sister, I do not have the authority to make decisions contrary to what I see on my screen. When questions are necessary, I will receive notice to proceed with questions. If your answers necessitate a discussion, I will be given the wisdom to make recommendations to you that will enlighten your understanding. Then you can make the right decisions for the good of your soul. Because questions have been waived in your case, the only recommendation I can make is to instruct you to proceed to Checkpoint Three.

"Oh, I see. Well then, I will continue on my journey home and pray for you as I go. Thank you."

14

Chaos

Deciding to make a fast trip back to the entrance to the road to Heaven, Tommy also wanted to make sure he wouldn't miss anything when Sister Mary Ann reached Checkpoint Three.

"It looks like traffic is slowing down considerably so I'll just make a quick run back to the entrance to make sure no one else in on the way, then I'll race to catch up to Sister Mary Ann."

Approaching Checkpoint One, Tommy could see there was no angel at the desk. The gate was down and nobody was in sight.

"Wow! What's going on? No angel and no people. I'll just continue to the entrance, but if I don't see anyone I'm not going to go home before I watch Sister Mary Ann either go to Heaven or to the waiting room."

As Tommy rounded the final turn before reaching the entrance, he was shocked to see the angel waking towards him and a crowd of people sitting down on the road near the entrance.

"What's happening angel?"

"We have a problem with a soul not wanting to proceed and he's holding up three people with many more souls on the way."

"What are you going to do?"

"I'm calling in a supervisor."

As the angel made her way back to her desk Tommy slowly proceeded toward the entrance. Stopping fifty feet from Billy, who was sitting on the ground talking to the doctor, Tommy knew they couldn't see him, so he decided to listen to their conversation.

"So, doc, what's your name?"

"My name is Samuel, but my friends call me Sam. Billy, let's be serious. You can't go home because you're dead, and your feet won't walk in that direction anyway. Plus, you're preventing all the rest of us from getting to Heaven."

"Doc, I made a big mistake by taking drugs for one last party. I was clean for two months and it looked like I was going to make it. But I'm young and I deserve another chance. I have always been a good person and always helped other people in any way I could. I even prayed and went to church once in awhile. If I could just speak to God for a few minutes, I'm sure I could convince Him to give me a break."

"It sounds to me like He already gave you a break by helping you stay clean for two months. Why should He give you another break?"

"Because I'm sorry and I really tried for two months. I asked Him every day to help me, and I thanked him every night before I went to sleep. So I messed up, so what? I didn't plan it. One minute I was at the party and the next thing I know is I'm dead. I didn't even have a chance to tell Him I was sorry. I just died - unexpectedly. This is definitely not cool."

"Well hurry up and speak to Him so we can move on."

"I will, as soon as I can figure out what to say. In the meantime why are you here? You don't look very old. Everyone else I passed on this road was old."

"I was in a car accident on my way home from work. I didn't die right away. I was pinned in the car and the fire rescue people couldn't get me out. I still had my phone with me so I called my wife to say goodbye. She told me to try and hang on and she would call a priest. She then jumped in her car and rushed to get to me in time. The priest arrived before she did, and he heard my confession and then gave me last rights. Unlike you, I had time to tell God I was sorry for my sinful life. I had actually been telling him I was sorry for several years. My wife had been preaching to me, for a long time, to change my behavior, and I finally took her advice. From that point on, I offered my services free to low-income people. Now I'm on my way to Heaven and I'm very anxious. I don't know what God will say to me."

"Why are you worried? You said you have been telling God you were sorry for your past sinful life and you have been helping the poor ever since. Don't you think He will be pleased with your change of heart?"

"Well, I wasn't exactly your run of the mill sinner. I was pretty bad."

"You don't look bad to me. I doubt you robbed any banks or killed anybody."

Sam was silent. He just looked at Billy and then at the ground.

"Excuse me, I'm Stephanie and this is Milton, and we would like to proceed to Heaven. Is there some kind of a problem I can help you with?

"Do you know God? I need special permission to return home. I don't like being dead."

"What is your name?"

"Billy."

"Billy, I can pray to God for you but I'm sure at this point He would prefer hearing directly from you".

"I don't know what to say".

"Speak the truth. God loves the truth."

15

Wow!

Pedaling as fast as he could, Tommy raced around the last turn before approaching Check Point Three. Back at the entrance he realized that the roadblock was not about to clear anytime soon, and he didn't want to miss Sister Mary Ann's outcome.

"Good news, I made it in time. There she is, just arriving at the angel's desk."

Tommy stopped pedaling and coasted to a position about ten feet from the angel. He didn't want to miss anything.

"Hello, I'm Sister Mary Ann and I am on my way to Heaven."

"Welcome Sister, we have been expecting you" the angel responded as he stepped away from his desk and began to kneel on the grass.

"Why are you kneeling down?" she asked as the day became much brighter, even though there was no sun in the sky. The angel didn't respond as he humbly began to smile and bow his head."

Slowly, a few feet from Sister Mary Ann, where the road came to an end, a warm light began to approach her. It grew in size until it reached the sky and completely encompassed her. She instantly became serene and could no longer see anything but the light. Smiling, and in obvious great peace, she whispered, "I love you too", as the light drew her and her tricycle toward itself. The moment she reached the light, the sky opened up and she was drawn up into an even greater light as the sound of beautiful voices could be heard singing in the far distance. Once she was completely out of sight, a large angel emerged from the light and approached the end of the road. With immensely large arms he drew the light to a close, returned the scene to its original condition, and abruptly disappeared. Tommy was speechless. The angel who was kneeling slowly stood up and returned to his desk. They exchanged glances but remained silent. After several minutes of peaceful reflection Tommy broke the silence...

"Excuse me. Was that Heaven?"

"Yes," the angel softly responded.

"Wow that was really, really moving. I mean, I don't know how to describe it. I just feel different. I feel peaceful … and kind of overwhelmed."

The angel smiled and looked away.

"Why did Sister Mary Ann's tricycle go with her into Heaven?"

"That is a very good question, Tommy, and I hope you will remember this answer for the rest of your life. Sister Mary Ann had a great childlike faith in God's love for her and for everyone else. She knew that her faith was a gift from God that she and every person receive from Him. Faith is a profound, deep, and intimate relationship with God that unites us to Him. Unfortunately, that faith can be weakened during the course of life because of the many distractions, worries, and temptations that confront all souls during their journey home to Heaven. It was Sister Mary Ann's childlike faith that united her to God and brought her to His arms so he could carry her Home to Heaven. Remember, Jesus said, "Amen, I say to you, unless you turn and become like children, you will not enter the kingdom of heaven" (Matt 18:3 NAB.)
Sister Mary Ann's tricycle was a representation of her childlike Faith and trust in God, and so it went with her to Heaven."

Tommy was quiet for a few moments, then looked at the angel and said, "I think I'll start heading home."

The angel smiled at Tommy and waved goodbye.

As Tommy slowly made his way back to the entrance, he could be overheard saying, "Wow! I never knew it would be like that. I don't know how to explain this to anyone."

16

Prayer is powerful

By the time Tommy reached the entrance, many of the people who had gathered around Billy were, unsuccessfully, trying to get him to move toward Heaven. Sitting on the ground, one after another, they began to relate their life stories to each other while they waited for the supervisor angel to arrive.

"Wow, I can't believe Billy is holding up all those people and he still won't move," Tommy thought as he moved closer to hear the conversation.

Suddenly, Stephanie stood up and asked for silence. As the conversation subsided, she turned to Billy and said, "Billy, you told us you were going to pray to God and ask for permission to go back home. There were four of us at the time, now there are ten and more are probably on the way. Nobody has perfect prayers; it's what is in your heart that matters. So, speak to God from your heart, you've waited long enough."

Billy was surprised by Stephanie's assertiveness. She wasn't his mother or teacher or employer, but nevertheless she basically ordered him to pray. Because he was somewhat of a rebel, he decided to challenge her in return.

"So, what makes you think you have a right to order me around, Stephanie?"

Immediately, everyone in the line to Heaven began to criticize and complain to Billy about his disrespect toward Stephanie.

"Billy, you have no right to speak to Stephanie that way, she is just trying to help you," complained Milton.

"I agree," Sam expressed as he stood up and moved away from Billy and closer to the building crowd.

"Oh wow, so now everyone is against me just because I don't accept orders to pray. And I don't even know anything about Stephanie, like how she died. For all I know she was robbing a bank."

As the crowd roared in complaint against Billy, a greater sound shook the ground which silenced everyone. Suddenly, a bright light approached and stopped next to Billy.

"Billy", a voice thundered as the light faded and an immensely large angel appeared. "Your heart is open to God, but your behavior is unacceptable in

His presence. Do not criticize Stephanie for it was her prayers that reached the heart of God on your behalf. She is not dead; she was in Church praying for the youth of the world who are addicted to drugs. And it is her love for God, and all of His children, which has earned you another chance at life. Almighty God wants you to go back, go back to the life you left in disgrace and be obedient to His will. Stephanie will counsel you and teach you His ways. Be respectful to her as God has placed you in her care."

The angel moved away, and a mighty wind began to blow as the light faded. Stephanie and Billy disappeared in a flash, leaving the crowd in silent amazement. Tommy was overwhelmed; so much was happening so quickly. Unsure of what to do, he just stared at the crowd and waited for the next development.

17

Return to Order

Now, that God had spoken through His angel, a greater sense of composure took hold of the souls in the line to Heaven. Everyone began to take their proper place according to the order in which they had arrived at the entrance. At the head of the line, Sam, turned and asked Milton to pray for him. He was visibly anxious and very apprehensive. As he began to walk slowly toward Checkpoint One, his anxiety increased with every step.

"What will God say to me? I've led a very bad life. Although for the last several years I have completely reformed my life and turned back to God, I'm sure I will have to give an accounting for my terrible sins. My sins were the worst of all sins."

As Sam rounded the last turn and stared at the straight away leading to Checkpoint One, he could see the angel sitting at the desk. In no rush to get there, he slowly approached the gate as her screen began to populate with all the data concerning Sam and his life.

"Good afternoon sir. Welcome to Checkpoint One. May I have your name?"

"Sam."

"Thank you for your answer Sam. I notice that you seem to be shaking a little bit. Actually, it is a pleasantly warm day. Is there a reason for your shaking?"

Sam's anxiety began to creep into his voice as he tried to answer.

"Well, I'm just a little nervous, I guess. I haven't had this experience before and I don't know what to expect."

"I understand Sam. Tell me a little bit about your life."

"Well, after college I went to medical school and then to my internship at a hospital so I could become board certified. While there I decided to specialize in Obstetrics and Gynecology. Eventually I opened my own OB/Gyn practice and was somewhat successful."

"I assume that means you brought many babies into the world."

"Uh, yes, yes I did. I brought babies into the world".

"How many?"

"Oh, I don't know. Many I guess."

"Sam's shaking increased as he seemed to back away from the angel's desk."

"Tell me Sam, does God love you?"

"Yes, God loves me."

"You're correct Sam. God does love you. And He wants you to be peaceful as you proceed on the road to Heaven. I'm going to raise the gate now and send you on your way to Checkpoint Two. Do you think you will be ok, or do you need an escort?"

"Who would be my escort?"

"Your guardian angel."

"Well, I'll give it a try by myself. If I need help, I'll ask at the next gate."

"Ok Sam. Have a good day."

As the gate rose, Sam, slowly and reluctantly, began walking to the next checkpoint. The somber look on his face, along with his anxiety, returned as he knew they both would.

18

God is merciful

Tommy wanted to follow Sam, but he knew that Milton, with his wagon full of bagels, would be going next so he decided to wait.

"I really want to see what will happen to Sam; he seems so worried. But since Milton is leaving now, I'll follow him until he passes Checkpoint One; then I'll catch up to Sam."

Milton's joy at the prospect of seeing his wife encouraged him to walk as fast as possible towards the first turn in the road. Once he rounded the turn, and believed he was out of sight of the people back at the entrance, he started to run pulling his wagon full of bagels behind him.

"I can't wait to see you, Teresa. I'm on my way."

As Milton ran toward Heaven, Tommy raced past him toward the checkpoint so he could position himself behind the angel's desk. He didn't want to miss anything. Ten minutes later as Milton approached the gate, the angel stood and welcomed him with a warm smile.

"Milton, welcome to Checkpoint One. I've been reading about you. It seems you have led a very kind and generous life."

"I have tried. It wasn't always easy. Many times, I was exhausted taking care of my wife, Teresa, when I was still going to work every day. But when I retired it became much easier."

"I don't have any questions for you, although I know the next two checkpoints most likely will."

"What kind of questions will they have?"

"I'm not sure, but possibly questions about your relationship with God. Questions like, did you pray, did you attend church, did you teach your children about God, do you love God. Do you believe He loves you? You know just general questions like that."

"Oh."

"And unless you have any questions for me Milton, I will raise the gate and send you on your way."

"Uh ... no... no I don't have any questions."

As the angel raised the gate, Milton took off running like a racehorse out of the starting gate. Running around turn after turn, memories of his wife filled his mind with the happiness he had long forgotten. Suddenly, as he approached the last turn, just before he would see the Checkpoint, he spotted Sam sitting by the roadside.

Out of breath, he slowly approached Sam who seemed to be just staring at the ground. Sam briefly looked up at Milton and then without saying a word, looked back at the ground.

"Sam, what's going on?"

"I'm too afraid to proceed."

"Sam, I prayed for you as you asked. What are you afraid of?"

"God's judgment."

"Sam, God is merciful and forgives us our sins if we tell Him we are sorry and intend to avoid sin in the future."

"I did tell Him I am sorry, and I have lived a good life for many years since my terrible sins were committed. But my sins were so bad I can't forgive myself and the thought of facing God and giving an accounting of my life just terrifies me."

"Sam, I was born Jewish, and when I married my wife Teresa, she explained to me what being a Christian was all about. But because of my upbringing in a large Jewish family, I remained a Jew for many years after I was married. Then, one day, my sister became very ill and was dying. She kept repeating over and over again 'How do I know I am forgiven; how do I know I am forgiven?' I didn't know what to tell her, so I asked Teresa. She told me to tell her about Jesus whose suffering and death on the cross was payment for our sins."

"So, I told my sister and she said that Jesus was just a man and that only God can forgive sins."

"I informed Teresa and she agreed to speak with my sister. We went over there together, and Teresa explained that God presents Himself to us in three different ways. He is God the Father, God the Son, and God the Holy Spirit. He is One God in Three Persons. She told my sister that just as I am her brother, I am also a son, and I am also a husband, and I am also a friend to many people. But still, I am one person. She said it is the same with God. He is one God in Three Divine Persons. He is our Father and Creator in Heaven, Jesus our Redeemer on earth, and the Holy Spirit our Comforter who remains with us until we get back home to Heaven. Teresa then prayed with my sister and the next day my sister accepted Jesus as her Savior and died peacefully. I was very impressed by that and a few weeks later I too accepted Jesus as my Savior, and I became a Christian. Since then, I have come to know Jesus, who really is God, and my life has become very happy and fulfilled. I don't think my love for my wife would ever have grown to the extent that it has if I had not been communicating daily in prayer with God. And my communicating with God has been a direct result of my conversion."

"Milton, I understand what you are saying. I was born a Christian and always prayed to God. When I graduated from college, I married my wife and she helped me get through medical school by working two jobs. After my internship, at a hospital, I opened my own practice. Business was very slow at first and paying the rent and the nursing staff became a serious problem. So, I started doing abortions at a nearby abortion clinic and my life deteriorated quickly. I no longer prayed, my wife became very upset, and our relationship suffered badly. When my children learned about it, they wanted to leave home. That upset my wife so much she demanded that I stop doing abortions or she and the children would leave me. That very day I stopped, and I begged God to forgive me. I also prayed and asked Him to help my practice grow so I could make ends meet. He did help me, and my practice became successful. But that was only after I had spent five years aborting more than eleven thousand babies. Now I have to face God and possibly all those babies. While I know God has forgiven me, I can't forgive myself. I can't even look in the mirror without hating myself. It is a terrible burden I live with every day."

"Sam, tell me about some of the good things you have done in your life."

"Well, for the last fifteen years I have treated low-income women free of charge. My practice has grown, and I have managed to get word out to nurses who work in the abortion clinic that if they ever want to leave that business I will hire them. Several have done so. But the thought of thousands of dead babies haunts me every day. Sometimes I still have nightmares. Years ago, I had nightmares every night. I can't shake the memory of my sinful life."

"In spite of all that, God still loves you Sam. And He has forgiven you even though you can't forgive yourself. It is time to forgive yourself and go to God, we are on the road to Heaven."

"Ok, Milton. I'll give it another try."

As Sam began to walk toward Checkpoint Two, Milton decided to sit by the roadside so as not to interfere with Sam's private interview with the angel. In the meantime, Tommy rode ahead to his usual vantage point to await the arrival of Sam.

"I know there are other people getting started at the entrance, but I can't miss this situation with

Sam. He says he knows God loves him and has forgiven him but yet he is still afraid to see God. That doesn't make sense."

19

Fear is useless;
What is needed is trust

Sam approached Checkpoint Two at a snail's pace. Even during the many years he had helped the poor, Sam's anxiety for his past life had tormented him. Now fifty feet away from what could be the beginning of his judgment, the angel at the desk called out to him and waved him on.

"It's ok Sam; you're safe; we'll just chat for a few minutes."

Sam arrived at the desk and was so overwhelmed with fear that the angel offered him his seat behind the desk. As he sat down, he found himself looking at the angel's computer screen. And there it was, in living color, the horrible reality of his past, right in front of him. The angel noticed but didn't say anything. Thirty seconds past, and in that time Sam didn't see anything that he had not already asked God to forgive.

"It's all there, everything in my past that I ever did, good or bad. It says that every sin I committed

I have already asked God to forgive. And it says right here that I accepted all of God's forgiveness. So why am I still afraid of God's judgment?"

The angel approached the desk.

"Scroll to the next page Sam. What you will be looking at is the present. This is the condition of your soul at present. This is what you need to repent of and ask God to forgive. That is why you didn't see it on the first page. It's not your past, it's the present."

Sam stared at the screen in silence. A minute passed, and without comment he stood up and walked toward the gate. His trembling seemed to have disappeared. He was calm but didn't look toward the angel.

"You can leave it here, Sam, if you wish. You can't bring it to Heaven."

Sam was obviously disturbed and not responding to the angel.

"It's up to you Sam."

A few minutes passed and Sam's silence continued, prompting the angel to open the gate.

As he walked toward Checkpoint Three, Tommy followed, silently praying for Sam.

20

Courage

Melissa was next in line. At 64 she was one year away from retirement when fire swept through her apartment building, sending her racing down the fire escape and into the street. Because the fire alarm was so loud, she was one of the first to make it out of the burning building. As she looked back at the flames beginning to emerge from some of the balconies, she noticed a small boy screaming from the third floor. His mother was unable to open the door to the hall way. Melissa knew that the fire escape was at the end of every hallway on the side of the building. Screaming to the boy to stay where he was, she charged to the fire escape on the ground level and raced to the second floor. Hoping that the flames had not yet reached the second floor, she swung open the door and raced to the apartment just below the little boy's third floor balcony. As she banged on the door, an elderly man opened it and asked for help. She directed him to the fire escape and ran through the apartment to the balcony. Looking up, she instructed the boy to hang from the balcony railing and she would climb up on her railing and rescue him. The moment she grabbed him, the boy's mother appeared on the balcony hysterically screaming that the flames were inside her apartment. Melissa instructed the boy to run through the apartment to the fire escape and down to the street. Turning to help his mother, she was surprised to see that she was already hanging from the balcony. As Melissa reached up to help the boy's mother, she suddenly let go, sending Melissa and herself crashing to the ground. Two weeks later,Melissa woke from her coma in the city hospital with multiple spinal cord injuries. Completely paralyzed from the neck down, she faced a grim future without surgery. With a 50/50 chance that the surgery would be successful Melissa decided to go ahead even though there was a small risk that she could lose her life. She lost the gamble and was now approaching Checkpoint One.

"Good afternoon. Welcome to Checkpoint One. May I have your name? "

"Yes, my name is Melissa."

"Thank you, Melissa. I have a few questions for you. The first question is: Do you believe in God's mercy, His forgiveness?"

"Yes, I do, and I have shared that truth with many hurting people."

"Have you accepted God's forgiveness in your own life?"

"Yes, I have, although I still do have great sorrow for my sins."

"I see in your report that you had a great struggle to turn back to God, but once you did, you persevered."

"I have persevered, and it was because of God's mercy. I was abused at a very young age and it turned my life into a nightmare. But with the help of some very dedicated people, I was successful in finding God and freedom from my sinful life. My sorrow at having offended God, for so many years, never left me."

"You do realize that God is very happy with your repentance, do you not?"

"Yes, I do, but I also think that when I see Him I will be speechless and filled with sorrow and shame and not feel worthy to even look at Him. I get emotional just thinking about it."

As Melissa wiped a tear from her eye, the angel raised the gate.

"Be peaceful, Melissa. God's mercy comes from His immense love for you. Have a good day."

21

Love is Patient

Milton decided that he had waited long enough and started walking to Checkpoint Two.

"I'm sure Sam would have finished by now and is on his way to the last checkpoint."

As he rounded the turn, he spotted Sam going through the gate and heading to Check Point Three. Minutes later Milton was greeted by the angel.

"Welcome Milton, I've been expecting you."

"Thank you. The first Angel told me you would probably have some questions for me."

"Actually, I don't have any of the usual questions, but I do have one request for you."

"Sure, go ahead."

"Sam is just ahead of you and is proceeding to his last checkpoint. He needs to make a major decision so he can finally find peace. I ask that you pray for him."

"I will."

"Thank you"

The angel raised the gate, and Milton was on his way pulling his wagon full of bagels behind him.

22

Perfect Love drives out fear

Sam struggled to keep walking to the last checkpoint. He felt more alone than at any time in his life. He had listened to Milton and his advice, his wife and her prayers, the priest who gave him last rights, and even one of the EMT's who tried to free him from the wreckage. But in spite of all those prayers and genuine concern, he couldn't shake his fear of God's judgment. Tommy had already raced ahead to the gate to await Sam's arrival. With the angel and the gate in view, Sam started looking for a possible glimpse of Heaven and God. Seeing nothing; he slowly approached the desk.

"Hello, I'm Sam and I'm as ready as I'll ever be for whatever awaits me."

"Welcome Sam. Before we begin, I have one fundamental question for you; do you love God?"

"Yes!"

"Then I want to remind you of what you have heard in church many times. 'Eye has not seen, ear has not heard, nor has it entered into the heart of man what God has prepared for those who love Him."

"I remember that, and yes, I have heard it many times. But in spite of that, I have continued to be afraid of God's judgment. And I never knew the reason why; that is, until I arrived at Checkpoint Two. The angel's computer said that I have on-going resentment and un-forgiveness. But it didn't say who or what my un-forgiveness and resentment is directed towards. And it didn't say why that would make me afraid of God's judgment. It did say, however, that I had forgiven myself for my sins because I knew that God had forgiven me. That was quite a surprise because I always thought that because I couldn't forgive myself that possibly God had not forgiven me either, even though I had already accepted His forgiveness. But now I see that there must be someone else I haven't forgiven. And I don't know who."

"Ok Sam, let's go back to your medical school days and the many types of instruction and training which you received. Aside from the strictly medical aspects of your training, you also received in-depth psychological training which helped you understand the correlation between the mind and the body. This is sometimes referred to as 'mind over body'. That particular training helped you to clearly see the effect your thoughts have on your body. And that effect can contribute to the physiological aspect of human behavior. In your case, your fear of God's judgment caused you to tremble at the first and second checkpoints. During the course of your life, you had serious resentment toward yourself and un-forgiveness toward your wife. And you still have both. Can you think for a moment and see if you can discover why?"

"Serious resentment toward myself, and un-forgiveness for my wife … Wow! I can't imagine why. I love my wife."

"Sam, you married your wife after college and then in your last year of medical school she became pregnant just before your graduation. After graduation, you enrolled in an internship at the local hospital. Because of your specialty, you routinely delivered newborns in the maternity department. Three months later, your wife announced she did not want the child because she would have to stop working and you both needed the income. She asked you to perform an abortion at home. You refused and she threatened to go to the local abortion clinic. In spite of your pleas to save your child, she would not change her mind and insisted you abort the baby, or she would go to the clinic. You reluctantly agreed and aborted your own son at 13 weeks. Even though you continue to love your wife, you have never forgiven her. And you have resented yourself for that un-forgiveness because you know that you can't expect God to forgive you if you can't forgive your wife. In other words, you are standing in your own way of peace with God. Yes, you have asked God to forgive you for killing your own child, and all those you later killed in abortion. But you still retain the guilt of not forgiving your wife and you have not asked God to forgive you for that because it is ongoing, and you have not repented of it. You have also buried it in your subconscious which is why you continue to wonder why you fear God's judgment."

Sam was dumfounded – speechless. He just stared at the angel and shook his head.

"Are you saying that all these many years of fearing God and resenting myself could have been avoided if I had just forgiven my wife?"

"Yes, and you probably would not have killed other babies at the abortion clinic. You would have worked part time for another physician or the local hospital. Your bitterness, and un-forgiveness of your wife, has caused all of your problems. And, as you remember, she repented shortly after her abortion and asked for your forgiveness. You never gave it to her. In spite of that, she forgave you and continued to love you. She knew how much the abortion hurt you."

Sam was silent once again, this time with tears running down his face. He knew what he had to do to remove his fear of God's judgment.

"Sam, God knows you love Him. And he remembers all the good you have done for many years. He also knows that your love for your wife really does exist, but your lack of forgiveness for her is causing you to look away from Him. A clear conscience makes it possible to see God face to face. Your conscience is suffering and needs your cooperation. You must forgive your wife."

"I need some time to think about it. I'm sure I will eventually forgive her, but the hurt of killing my own child is still unbearable."

"Sam, across the street is a gate to the waiting room. You can think about your life and your relationship with God there. Remember, your wife is a human being also. She has had her own struggles. Be merciful to her just as you want God to be merciful to you."

Sam nodded, wiped the tears from his eyes, and crossed the street to the waiting room.

Tommy waited silently for Sam to be out of sight; he had questions for the angel.

"Excuse me, why did my prayers not work? I prayed for Sam to make the right decisions so he could go to Heaven."

"Sam has a free will, Tommy, and God does not interfere with a soul's free will. He gives the soul all the necessary graces to combat temptation, but he doesn't prevent the soul from making the wrong choice. That choice is the soul's decision. Sam did not respond positively to God's grace."

"It must be very sad for God to have people ignore Him. Have you ever spoken with God about that?"

"We angels, and all the Saints in Heaven, are in union with God; we are united by His love. When He is offended, we are offended. When He hurts, we hurt. We are the family of God, a pure family. Sam's rejection of God's grace hurt us all. You are correct Tommy, it is very sad for God when His children, whom He loves so much, ignore Him.

23
Eternal Reward

Tommy was aware that many people were arriving at the entrance, but he couldn't pull himself away from the arrival of Milton who would be approaching the last checkpoint at any moment.

"I see him. He's coming around the turn now. And he still has his wagon full of bagels. He probably doesn't know that he can't bring them into Heaven."

As Milton approached the Angels desk, the gate slowly began to rise and the bright light from Heaven appeared once again. The angel knelt down next to Tommy and Tommy followed suit. As the angel bowed his head, Tommy watched Milton raise both his hands toward the sky as the light grew larger and brighter. An amazing smile of peace and joy captured Milton's face as he was drawn into the light and lifted up into Heaven. A warm wind blew down upon Tommy and the Angel as Tommy experienced a peace that quietly consumed him. For several minutes, the light remained and then gradually faded as Tommy slowly regained his strength and the angel moved back to his desk.

"Gee, I hadn't expected that. It happened so fast, and I didn't see the very large angel that we saw last time."

"It's different every time Tommy. Milton had completely surrendered his life to God many years ago. There was no need for me to ask him any questions or even converse with him. He lived in God and God lived in him."

"I thought that surely he would have to leave his wagon and the bagels here. But that didn't happen."

"Do you remember Sister Mary Ann and her tricycle going to Heaven? She didn't leave it here because it represented her childlike faith in God. Well, it is the same with Milton. The wagon and the bagels were representative of his faithful love for his wife. And surely love is most welcome in Heaven."

"I better get going back to the entrance, there will be people on their way here and I don't want to miss anything. By the way, when you have some time, will you please explain to me what the waiting room is all about?"

"Sure, just remind me."

24

Victim

Just as Melissa was rounding the last turn before Checkpoint Two, Tommy raced past her on his way to the entrance. Surprised to see Melissa, he abruptly stopped and waited for her to pass. Knowing that she couldn't see him, he turned around and followed her to the Gate.

"Wow, I missed her at the first gate and have no information at all. I'll have to listen carefully, so I know what to pray for."

"Welcome, Melissa, I have been expecting you. I see from your responses at the first checkpoint that you have expressed true sorrow for your sinful life and have accepted God's forgiveness. That is good news. Have you forgiven yourself?"

Melissa was surprised by the question and became momentarily silent as she searched for an answer.

"Well, actually... I've never really considered that. I mean... I don't know the answer. I just haven't given it any thought."

"You also said you think that when you see God you will be speechless and filled with sorrow and shame and not feel worthy to even look at Him."

"Yes, I did say that, and I imagine I will be ashamed of myself when I see God face to face."

"Knowing and believing that God has forgiven you, do you think He will want you to be ashamed in front of Him?"

"I don't know."

"Do you think God made a mistake by forgiving you?"

"No. He knows of my sincere sorrow."

"Well, if God did not make a mistake by forgiving you, then you must be saying He did the right thing."

"Yes, He did."

"In other words, you agree with God."

"I do."

"Well now that you agree with God for having forgiven you, would it make good sense for you to forgive yourself?"

Melissa attempted to answer but lost her voice as tears formed in her eyes. Granting her all the time she needed, the angel silently waited for an answer.

Composing herself, just enough to speak, Melissa struggled with her answer. "If you knew what my sins were, you would understand why it is so difficult for me to forgive myself."

"I do know of your sins Melissa. Your life is right in front of me on my computer screen."

Realizing this was the moment she needed to unburden herself of her guilt, Melissa took a deep breath and started to speak, but suddenly stopped and said, "I feel weak and need a moment." The angel immediately brought his chair into the street and offered it to her. Once she was comfortable, she continued: "When I was five years old, I was abused by my aunt. She was my mother's sister. This continued until I was ten. When I entered middle school, and made new friends, one of the older girls abused me just as my aunt had. By the time I was in high school, I was sexually disoriented and had many girl-friends. College was the same and my life was very sinful. All during this time, my conscience was very heavy with guilt. I didn't know God because my home life was never religious. Immediately after my twenty-seventh birthday, I had a nervous breakdown. My life was tortured and I didn't know what to do about it. That was when God arranged for me to watch a religious television program at the mental health center. I was very moved by what I heard, and once I was released from the mental health center, I joined a church and committed my life to Jesus. For the past thirty-seven years, I have been a guest speaker for countless organizations and churches, where I bring the truth about sexual disorientation to the youth of the world. Many young people have been saved from a life of misery and shame and brought into the joy of God's presence because of this mission which God has given me. But for some reason, in spite of my devotion to God, accepting His forgiveness, and leading a new life according to His will, I continue to hold onto my guilt. I can't seem to forgive myself. It makes no sense."

"Melissa, it is obvious that you love God. And you are aware that He loves you. But your memory of offending him for so many years won't leave you. When God forgives you of your sins, He also sends you His healing grace. Your sins are not only forgiven but the harm those sins have caused to your soul is healed. Subconsciously, you are not accepting that healing because you don't believe you are worthy of it. And that is because you remember your sinful offenses against God whom you love. It pains you to even think about it. Melissa, you have one more checkpoint to go through. I will pray for you while you're on your way, in the hope that you will ask God for the grace to accept His healing."

As Melissa passed through the gate, she had a greater sense of hope then she ever had experienced in her life. She now had something to look forward to.

25

Everyone's Future

Tommy realized he was falling behind and decided to hurry back to the entrance to see who would be next. His plan was to then race back to Checkpoint Three and witness Melissa going to Heaven or to the waiting room. As he travelled, his sense of praying for Melissa was paramount. If he had learned anything on this very unusual day of his life, he learned that prayer is vital for every human being.

"Dear Lord Jesus, I know that I am not dead, so I hope my prayers will work. Melissa is very upset, and I hope she calms down enough to be close to you and accept your healing. Please help her. Thank you."

As he cleared the last turn, Checkpoint One came into view and Tommy was shocked to see so many people in line. Already at the angel's desk was an elderly man who was answering questions. Behind him was a middle-aged woman, behind her was a clergyman, behind him was a small young boy, maybe five or six years of age, and more people approaching the entrance. Riding up to the desk he overheard the angel speaking, "I'm sorry Klepto, but you absolutely cannot bring all of that stuff into Heaven. As a matter of fact, you can't bring any of it with you to Heaven."

"Why not?"

"The rules don't permit it and I don't make the rules."

"Well, who does? This is all my stuff and I can't part with it."

"We can get to that in a minute, but first, what is your real name? I don't have a Klepto in my system."

"My regular name, which I haven't used for years, is Bradley. But all my friends call me Klepto."

"Why do your friends call you Klepto?"

"They call me Klepto because I'm a kleptomaniac."

"I see. Well, just one moment while I search the data base...there we are, I found you, Bradley Carstairs, age 83."

"That's me. Now please open the gate. I'm in a hurry. I'm on my way to Heaven."

"Just a reminder Bradley, when you get to the next Checkpoint, you will not be allowed to bring that stuff with you into Heaven."

"I'll cross that bridge when I get to it. You never know, maybe the next angel will make an exception. In the meantime, I prefer that you call me Klepto. I never really liked the name Bradley."

"The angel raised the gate and waited for Bradley to be out of sight and then whispered into her intercom, "Hey, Number Two, there's another one of those special types on the way."

26
Freedom

Tommy raced around the turn after flying past Checkpoint Two heading for Number Three. He didn't want to miss Melissa and her moment of truth; a truth he hoped would finally take hold in her heart and release her from her self imposed imprisonment in guilt. As the last turn came into view, he spotted Melissa approaching it. He coasted up beside her and remained a few feet away as he silently prayed for her. Rounding the turn, she began to audibly pray. "Dear Lord Jesus, I have accepted your mercy and forgiveness but the thought of hurting you all of those years is too painful to bear. I need your healing; please heal my memory and free me from this guilt. My sorrow is real but the memory of all those sins is a burden I can't carry any longer."

Tommy noticed that tears were flowing down Melissa's face as she seemed to walk faster toward the end of the road. With about 200 feet remaining, Melissa started to run, "Jesus, Jesus, save me," she yelled as she raised her hands in the air, "I love You, I accept your mercy and healing, I release all my guilt to you."

As her speed increased, a miraculous smile appeared on her face and an immense light appeared at the end of the road racing toward Melissa. Suddenly, the light met Melissa in a brilliant flash, which knocked Tommy off his bicycle. As he looked up, Tommy could see Jesus embrace Melissa and race her upward to Heaven, surrounded by hundreds of angels, as beautiful music filled the sky. The light remained for several minutes until the music began to fade. Tommy looked toward the gate and could see the angel kneeling. Picking up his bicycle, he started walking to the angel's desk. Slowly the angel stood.

"Wow. That was awesome. Have you ever seen that happen before?"

"Yes, I have Tommy. When a soul surrenders to God, there is much joy in Heaven. Melissa completely surrendered to God and finally experienced the joy He had been trying to give her for many years."

"Do the people who go to the waiting room go to Heaven like that? That was awesome."

"Each soul's return to God is different. Each person's relationship with God is unique to that person. You saw the joy on Melissa's face as she ran to meet Jesus. What you didn't see was the joy in God's heart. God had his child back home, safe and sound. There are no words to explain His happiness when souls accept His mercy, forgiveness and healing. Melissa's happy face was just a small reflection of God's joy."

"When Milton reached Heaven, I asked you to tell me about the waiting room. Is this a good time?"

"Sure. Do you have any specific questions?"

"Well, I have seen that most people who go there have some sort of a problem they have not completely dealt with. What happens when they get there?"

"In the waiting room, souls begin to see themselves as they really are. They see those things about themselves that they never wanted to look at before. They see their weaknesses, their resentments, their selfishness, vanities, and pride. But they also begin to see the reasons for their failings. Sometimes it was hurt they endured, sometimes it was revenge in their hearts, sometimes it was a lack of turning to God for forgiveness and asking for His help. But in all of those situations in their lives where they did not live according to God's will, they will see that they always had God's grace available to help them but rejected it in favor of their own will. This will be a source of sadness for them because they will begin to feel God's presence with them, and as time goes by, they will begin to have a glimpse of God in Heaven. The longer they are in the waiting room, their sadness will increase because their love for God will grow and they will not be able to join Him in Heaven. Their greatest suffering will come when they realize that God sees something within them that displeases Him. All souls will eventually want to turn their hearts completely toward God, admit every weakness, and repent and reject those weaknesses forever. They will come to accept that they must decrease and God must increase in their hearts. Their final prayer will be to ask God to help them love Him completely. The entire process will be one of learning and growing in honesty and truth before God."

"Do most people go to Heaven or to the waiting room?"

"That is a question I cannot answer for you, Tommy, because I don't have the statistics."

Tommy knew there was a place called hell, but he didn't want to ask the angel about that, at least not now.

"Thank you, Angel Number Three. I better get back to the entrance; many more people are on their way here."

27

Disbelief

Racing to the entrance, Tommy passed Bradley on his way to Checkpoint Two. Bradley had stopped by the roadside to rest because his many possessions were too heavy to carry for any long distance. He had bags filled with jewelry, clothing, cell phones, check books, cash, gold coins, cameras, anything of value he was able to steal and not be discovered. Realizing that Bradley would not be able to travel quickly, Tommy decided to proceed to the entrance, confident he would be able to return in time before Bradley was able to reach the checkpoint. As he arrived at the entrance, Tommy could hear the angels greeting.

"Hello, and welcome to Checkpoint One. May I have your name?"

"My name is Susan."

"Thank you, Susan. I have a few questions for you. Are you a forgiving person?"

"Yes."

"Do you believe in God?"

"No."

"At any point in your life did you believe in God?"

"When I was a small girl, I believed there might be a God; but later on in life I came to realize that was probably just wishful thinking. Today I am an atheist."

"And what is your age?"

"I am forty-seven."

"What was your career in life?"

"Until last week I was a Governor in the United States. I had a stroke five days ago and this morning the doctors were unable to save me, so here I am."

"Did you see the sign at the beginning of the road?"

"Yes, it said 3 Miles to Heaven."

"Do you know anything about Heaven?"

"I know what people say about Heaven, but I don't believe it."

"What do you think it will be like in Heaven?"

"I don't think there is a Heaven."

"You said that when you were a youngster, you believed there might be a God, but later on in life you came to realize that was probably just wishful thinking. Did that mean that you wished there was a God?"

"When I was little, my mother and father were killed in a car accident and I was placed in a foster home. The foster mother and father were mean to me. They never went to church or spoke of God. In school, my friends had parents who took them to church, but their parents never asked me to join them. By the time I attended college, hardly anyone spoke about God. In my senior year I married but my marriage ended in divorce two years later. My husband had been unfaithful to me, and he had no intention of changing. He also was an atheist and convinced me there was no God. If there was a God, why did He let all those bad things happen to me? The answer is, there is no God."

"What happened after your divorce?"

"I had my first real break in life. I was hired by a newspaper as a reporter and was paid very well. I became interested in investigative reporting and I spent several years uncovering political corruption in government. Eventually, I became an editor of the newspaper and wrote editorials against political corruption. One of the political parties asked me to run for public office. I accepted and six months later, I was elected and became a state senator. Several years later, I was elected governor."

"Do you have any regrets about your time as governor in your state?"

"Probably only one, but that's all in the past."

"Would you like to talk about it?"

"Not really. It wouldn't do any good."

"If it could do some good, what would you hope for?"

"Oh, I don't know; maybe a clear conscience."

"Do you think that if you did talk about it, it would help to clear your conscience?"

"Well, I have talked about it to myself for years and it never did any good. Why would talking to someone else about it accomplish anything?"

"You can get their feedback, which sometimes can help you see the situation more clearly. They can also make recommendations, which could steer you in the right direction so you can receive the help you need to unburden your soul."

"Unburden my soul? I never thought about having a soul. A conscience, yes, but a soul is a typically religious expression and I never participated in any religion."

"Your soul is given to you by God when He creates you. All the good you do is reflected in your soul. Same with the sins you commit. Confessing your sins to God with the intention of not repeating them and expressing your sorrow for having offended Him is called repentance. When you repent of your sins and ask God to forgive you, He does, and He restores your soul to its pure state. When that happens, your conscience is freed from its guilt and you have a fresh start."

"Interesting. So what's next? Where do I go from here?"

"We can discuss this regret that you have, or you can think about it and proceed to the next Checkpoint. Hopefully you will discuss it there. The choice is yours."

"I'll think about it."

"I will raise the gate for you Susan. Have a nice day."

28

Crumbs

Tommy raced past Susan knowing that Bradley was about a half mile ahead sitting by the roadside. Coasting around the last turn, he spotted Bradley picking up his cargo and starting to walk to the Checkpoint.

"Gee, I wish I could help him carry that load of stuff. He seems so overwhelmed."

Tommy knew very well that he was unable to be seen by or communicate with the people on the road to Heaven. The angels could see and speak with him, but any help he wanted to offer the people could only be communicated through prayer. Bradley was walking so slowly that Tommy had to get off his bicycle and walk beside him as they began to approach the gate. With less than fifty feet remaining, Bradley suddenly dropped his stuff on the grass along the edge of the road and sat down.

"Sir, you can check in over here by the gate."

Responding to the angel Bradley shouted back, "Relax...I need a few minutes to rest. I have a lot of stuff and it's heavy."

Tommy became concerned that Susan would not be able to continue because Bradley was blocking the way to the checkpoint. Unable to speak to Bradley, he pedaled over to the angel.

"Excuse me, a woman is about to arrive any moment and won't be able to pass Bradley. Is there anything you can do?"

"I need to give him every opportunity to make his own decisions. This is a critical moment for him. Unless he decides to permanently block the road, our policy is to give him all the time he needs."

As Tommy turned to pedal back to Bradley, Susan came around the far turn and began to approach them. Bradley noticed and began to pick up his many bags of stolen goods and slowly walked toward the angel's desk.

"Welcome Bradley. You have quite a load there."

"Actually, it's not as big as some I've had during my lifetime. When I was younger, I usually had much bigger loads. But before we go any further, I would prefer you call me by my regular name, which is Klepto."

"The only name on my screen is Bradley so I must address you by that name. And I'm aware that you were informed at the last Checkpoint that you are not permitted to bring your stuff into Heaven. But you insisted that you must bring it with you. Why do you insist on bringing it to Heaven?"

"I know many people who have died before me and I'm sure I'll meet them when I get there. Most of them liked me because I always had a lot of stuff. So, if I still have plenty of stuff, they will still like me. And I actually think that some of them loved me. And that's a lot better than being liked. So, I really need to keep my stuff and bring it with me."

"Bradley, all of your stuff was stolen from people. Many of them will be in Heaven. What will you say to them?"

"I'll just avoid them like all the other people I will avoid."

"What other people?"

"The people who were always criticizing me."

"Why were they criticizing you?"

"Because, according to them, I was stingy with my wealth. But the wealth they were talking about was the money my parents left me when they died. I had to hold on to as much of that as possible because it was the only thing I ever received from them, and now they are gone."

"What do you mean when you say, "the only thing?"

"My parents were very wealthy. They always traveled all over the world and rarely spent any time with me. I never received any love or affection from them. We had servants living in our home and they are the ones who were parents to me. When my real parents passed away, they left me more than seventy million dollars plus the house we lived in. I was forty six years old and I put the money in the bank so I could always have it as a reminder of my parents. The money became the love from them that I always wanted, but never received. Unfortunately, many people knew of my inheritance and they would make frequent requests for help. But because I didn't want to part with the money from my parents, I would sell some of the stolen stuff and give the money to whoever wanted it. But it never was very much and they would call me a miser. I never told them it was money from the stolen stuff. When I was young, I would steal stuff so I could have something to give to my friends so they would like me. When my parents died, I would steal stuff so I could sell it for money for food and expenses for the house. I was a major thief. But I always managed to steal much more than I needed and when I died, I had all this left over. Now I can use it to buy friends in Heaven. That way I'm guaranteed of being loved."

"I have information in front of me that says when you were fifty-one years of age you gave five thousand dollars to an orphanage. It then says that on Christmas of that year, you gave an additional one million dollars to that same orphanage. What caused you to depart from your plan of holding on to the money in the bank? And why did you not give the one million the first time?"

"That was an unusual situation. I met someone who told me he had been an orphan when he was nine years old and that the people who operated the orphanage were very kind and loving. He said that the orphanage frequently ran out of food and sometimes they had only one meal a day. But still he was happy because he felt wanted and loved. I asked if the orphanage was still operating. He said it had been twenty-five years since he lived there but he thought it probably would still be in existence. I looked it up and sure enough, they were still there. I went to see them and the director gave me a tour. I was surprised to see how desperate they were for everything needed to run an orphanage. Most of the beds were very old and in need of replacement. The playground equipment was dilapidated, and the pantry was very low on food supplies. But because of the loving atmosphere, I found myself wishing I had been there as a child instead of my own house where I had everything but love. I asked the director if I could make a donation and he was encouraged and said he would be happy for anything I could spare. I told him I would go to the bank in the morning and return with a five thousand dollar check. He was extremely grateful and said, "God Bless you." I'm not religious but I knew what he meant. A few weeks later, I ran into the same man who had been an orphan and I related to him what had happened. He was surprised at my generosity and said I should be proud of myself. He recalled something he had read about one of the popes, John Paul II, who said the poor need our help and that doesn't mean crumbs. I asked him what that meant. He said if someone was a billionaire, and gave one million dollars to charity then that would be crumbs to the billionaire. To be a billionaire, you would have to have at least one thousand million dollars. Then he said that I gave five thousand dollars and I was just a regular person. I never told him that I was a millionaire. That was in the summertime. For the next six months I kept thinking about my donation and I finally concluded that I had given crumbs to the orphanage. After all, just the playground equipment alone could cost five thousand dollars. My conscience really bothered me so by Christmas time I went back to the orphanage and gave them one million dollars. The director had tears in his eyes and said that now he would no longer have to tell the children they would not be having dinner as would frequently happen. Then he said a short prayer and asked God to bless me. When I drove home, something very unusual happened to me. I felt peaceful and sensed that God loved me. The next day I was planning on stealing but suddenly changed my mind. I looked at the woman whose purse I was about to steal and realized I would be hurting her. And since I had just helped the poor children I didn't want to start hurting people again. That night, I decided to try speaking with God. I didn't know any prayers but I asked Him to help me to stop stealing because I didn't want to hurt people anymore. I also told Him I was sorry for all my years of stealing and asked Him to forgive me. That was thirty three years ago and I haven't stolen since. I have also continued to help people financially and Isupport myself with my parents money which is just about all gone by now.

Suddenly, Susan, who had quietly arrived at the checkpoint and was standing behind Bradley interrupted and said, "Excuse me, may I ask a question?"

"Sure," the angel responded.

"Bradley, you said you were fifty-one when you made that immense donation to the orphanage. Did you feel a certain satisfaction and joy at being so kind and generous to the needy? Did it make you feel loved?"

"Actually, now that I think about it, yes it did."

"And since that time, you have continued to help the poor. And surely, that must have caused you to feel appreciated and loved. So, why then do you need to bring the stolen stuff to Heaven?"

"Because as my parents money diminished I became insecure thinking I had nothing left to buy love with. And the stolen stuff could not be returned because I never knew who owned it.

"Bradley," the angel interrupted "do you want to leave your stuff here and move on to Checkpoint Three, or do you still insist on bringing it with you?

"I'll move on. Possibly the next angel will have a better understanding of human nature and make an exception in my case."

"I will raise the gate for you Bradley. Have a nice day."

29

Stop the Silence

The priest approached the gate and greeted the angel. "Good morning. I'm Bishop Matthews."

"Good morning bishop and welcome to Checkpoint One. I have a few initial questions for you when you are ready."

"Do you mean there will be more questions later?"

"Yes. There will be questions at the next two checkpoints."

"I see. Well, please go ahead, I am ready."

"Have you been a responsible person?"

"Yes."

"Were you a good example to others?"

"I hope so."

"Were you judgmental?"

"No."

"Were you humble?"

"Yes."

"Did you always preach the truth even when you were criticized for concentrating too much on sin?"

"Well, that was many years ago. Back then I always preached against sin and emphasized leading chaste and holy lives. And there was support and also criticism for that type of preaching. In these more modern times, you don't want to turn people off, so we have toned that down considerably. It doesn't mean we are not preaching the truth. There is plenty of truth to preach. Love one another, forgive, help the poor, live the golden rule."

"What do you mean when you say 'we'?"

"I mean me and my brother priests and bishops. We don't want to lose parishioners by annoying them with the truth about modern society and sensitive topics, so we have toned it down. We can't pay the bills and keep the churches operating if we don't have a congregation making donations."

"What sensitive topics are you referring too?"

"Oh, you know, things like abortion, same sex marriage, contraception. Those are very controversial issues. So, we stay away from those things that upset people. We have a lot of families, and we want to keep them happy."

"Are all of the priests in your diocese on the same page with what to preach and what to be silent about?"

"All of the priests in my diocese know what the unwritten rules are and what topics to avoid. And they pretty much adhere to my preference. But I will definitely say that not all of them are on the same page. Some are very opposed to silence regarding those issues I mentioned. Some have even ventured into condemning those issues from the pulpit. But I and my loyal followers usually make our objections known very strongly and that usually keeps the vocal priests quiet for awhile. As I said, you don't want to upset the faithful. They're the ones who keep the lights on."

"Well, thank you Bishop for your candid answers. As I mentioned to you earlier, there will be two more Checkpoints ahead, each a mile apart. And there will be more questions and time for discussion when you arrive. I will raise the gate for you now. Have a nice day."

30

Searching for Truth

Susan's mind was racing back and forth between the past and the present as she tried to explain her situation to the angel at Checkpoint Two.

"Sure, I would like to unburden my conscience, but I need to do it logically, not with what has always proven to be fiction for me in my life."

"Susan, by regarding the existence of God as fiction, you are denying yourself the help you desperately need. You admit that nothing else you have tried has given you any help at all. You also admit that some of your friends have received help for various problems through prayer. And some of those problems were guilty consciences."

"I know, I know, I've heard it over and over again for years. But I never had any real proof."

"A good way to start is by identifying the problem. And I'm here to help you begin if you wish."

"Well, I'm sure you must have it on your screen, you told Bradley all about himself. Go ahead, I'll listen to your advice and give it some thought."

"Seven years ago, during your first term as Governor, you signed a death warrant for a man who murdered his wife. Prior to that time, you had granted clemency to three other inmates who had been convicted of murder. In each separate case, you commuted their sentence of death to a sentence of life imprisonment. In the case of the man whose death warrant you signed, he had divorced his first wife and then murdered his second wife. I have the real answer in front of me, but if you were to explain it in your own words, I'm sure it would lighten this burden you carry. You may take all the time you need. I'm here to listen if you wish to begin."

"Susan took a deep breath and said, "give me a minute will you, I need to collect my thoughts."

The angel waited patiently; he knew this would be difficult for her.

"Ok, I'll give it a try, but I don't see anything positive coming from my efforts; I've been down this road before. I sincerely loved my husband and assumed he loved me just as much as I loved him. Remember, my foster parents never loved me, so my stepping out of my hurt and trusting someone with the rest of my life was a major but very risky move. By the beginning of our second year of marriage, I sensed his love was no longer there, but I didn't know why. I never suspected adultery, I just assumed he didn't find me attractive anymore. Six months later, he announced he had had an affair. I was heartbroken. I concluded that I should at least be grateful for his honesty, forgive him and put it all behind us. He never said another word and I was beginning to heal. Three months later, he announced he wanted a divorce so he could marry the woman I thought he had stopped seeing. His betrayal was crushing. When I was hired by the newspaper, I buried myself in my work in an effort to ease the pain. It worked, I was over it...or so I thought. Years later, I painfully realized that it was not over. I found myself staring at a death warrant on my desk which I had agreed to sign after months of painful deliberation. One minute I wanted to commute the sentence to life imprisonment as I had done with three other inmates, and the next minute I wanted to sign the death warrant.

My secretary wanted to know why I was departing from my strong prolife position and I never gave her an intelligible answer. The reason, which I even tried to hide from myself, was I wanted revenge for what my husband had done to me. This inmate had divorced his wife and then killed another wife. My husband had divorced me and then killed my heart. It was the same thing and now I could get rid of the pain. I signed the death warrant and thought it was the end. It was not the end. The day they executed him, all the memories came back and now I have the added memory of having approved of the execution of a human being. "

Susan paused and wiped the tears from her eyes.

"The answer to your pain is God's mercy, Susan. Tell Him you are sorry and ask for His forgiveness. He loves you and wants your happiness even more than you do. He completely understands your situation. Let Him help you. He is ready and waiting to forgive you. Just ask Him."

Susan's tears didn't seem to be slowing down.

"You can approach God in prayer now, Susan, or move on to Checkpoint Three. Try to remember that you are God's child, and He loves you."

Unable to speak, Susan motioned to the angel to raise the gate. She waved goodbye in an obvious effort to say thank you.

31

Bribery

Tommy knew that he was missing the activity back at the entrance, but missing Bradley's arrival at the final checkpoint was unthinkable. Racing past Susan, he pedaled as fast as he could to catch Bradley. Rounding the final turn, he noticed half of Bradley's stuff by the side of the road and spotted Bradley just arriving at the gate with the other half.

"Welcome Bradley, you seem to be exhausted from your journey. Allow me to offer you my chair so you can rest a bit."

"No thank you, I'll be alright. Just give me a few minutes, I'll run back and get the rest of my stuff."

Moments later Bradley returned ... "On second thought, I think I will accept your offer to sit down and rest for a few minutes. I've been carrying this stuff for three miles. I can't wait till I get to Heaven so I can distribute it to all of my friends."

"Bradley, you will not be permitted into Heaven with your stuff."

"What's the big deal? I intend to share it with my friends. Sharing is a good thing, I'm very generous. I've been that way my entire life."
"Sharing is a good thing Bradley, you are correct. But sharing things to purchase love misses the point. Sharing is an expression of giving love; to help someone, to make their life more enjoyable. It is not meant to buy love. The love that one receives when giving to the needy, is God's love. When the giver opens his or her heart to God's inspiration to help a person in need, it is God's love that fills the giver and then flows to the one in need. The giver drawers closer to God and senses God's love for him, and he now begins to love himself. It is in the giving of love that one receives love. So, you don't need your stuff in Heaven because buying love is impossible. And besides, everyone in Heaven is completely happy anyway and they don't need anything."

"If what you say is true, then why do I still not feel loved?"

The only real love you experienced, was when you gave your parents' money to the orphanage and all the other people you helped for so many years. And that love was God's love which also caused you to love yourself."

"Well how am I ever going to feel loved if I'm dead now and can't give my parents' money to the poor?"

"Allow God to love you. You are a loveable person.   When you were a small child, you never felt your parents loved you, so you assumed you were not loveable. As a result, you have spent your life trying to buy love. You don't have to buy God's love; it is completely free. In fact, His love for you has existed since He created you. But no one ever told you. All you have to do is accept His love. He has been reaching out to you your entire life and He is reaching out to you right now. You have already told Him you were sorry for stealing everyone's stuff and you asked Him to forgive you. You always knew it was wrong but choose to remain in denial. Now it is time to accept His love for you.

Bradley became very quiet and pensive; he realized the angel was speaking the truth, the truth he never wanted to admit.

"Ok, I'll give it a try. Please forgive me Lord for not recognizing and accepting your love for me. I do now accept your love for me. Thank you, I accept your forgiveness."

"That was excellent Bradley. Now what do you intend to do with your stuff? As I mentioned, you can't bring it with you into Heaven."

"Well, I can't give it back to the people I stole it from because I'm dead. So, as long as I have it, I might as well give it to people in Heaven; there is no point in letting it go to waste."

"No Bradley, you must leave it here."

"All of it?"

"Yes!"

"Why"?

"Because, if you keep it, you are still putting your trust in stuff instead of God's love for you. And you have already told God you were sorry for not accepting His love. But now you are still relying on the value of things instead of the value of God's love and mercy for you".

"Okay, Okay, I will leave it. But I feel very insecure without my stuff."

"Across the street Bradley is a gate to the waiting room. You can go there and think about all of this."

"What will I be waiting for?"

"A change of heart."

32

Victims of Silence

Bishop Matthews approached the gate with curious anticipation. He knew there would be more questions and 'discussion' which the angel had spoken of. Just as he was about to introduce himself, Tommy raced around the turn and abruptly stopped at the desk. He was surprised to see someone so far ahead from the entrance.

"Good morning, I am Bishop Matthews."

"Good morning bishop and welcome to Checkpoint Two. I have a few questions for you."

"Yes, I was informed that you would have questions and possibly discussion. Please proceed, I am ready."

"You have mentioned that you didn't want to upset the parishioners by talking about sensitive topics. Why would they be upset?"

"Well, that would depend on the topic. There are some topics that are more sensitive than others. Probably the most sensitive would be abortion. If a priest discusses the topic of abortion, during his homily, he risks hurting those women in the congregation who have had abortions. Some of them he may very well have given pastoral counseling to in an effort to help them recover from their experience. In addition, when the priest speaks to the parishioners outside the church, after Mass, he is confronted with complaints from those who don't want to hear about abortion. Possibly some of them have experienced abortion themselves or maybe a family member. I have also been advised by some parishioners during my years as a priest, pastor, and now even as a bishop, that they would move to another Parish if I, or the other priests, didn't stop talking about abortion. And some of those parishioners were major donors."

"Did you ever think that some of those women in the congregation would be happy to hear homilies against abortion? Possibly they had an abortion themselves and want to forewarn other women, so they don't go down that same unhappy road. Surely you have heard many confessions and given counseling to women who have had abortions and you realize how much they suffer. Would not preventing the suffering that an abortion causes be a major concern of yours?

"Yes, it was always a major concern."

"Did you ever notice that some of your parishioners who had been attending Mass every week, for many years, were suddenly seeking counseling for their recent abortions? And did you consider that maybe they would not have had those abortions had you been preaching against it and advised them of the dangers and suffering it would cause them?"

"Well, yes, I did have thoughts about that from time to time. But frequently the criticism was very strong, and I didn't want to subject myself or my brother priests to such hostility."

"There were other topics that you avoided also. Same-sex marriage became legal in your country, but you never spoke a word against it."

"Oh yes, we definitely avoided that one. Some of the priests were homosexual and were familiar with other homosexuals in the diocese. They were afraid of having their secret revealed by their homosexual friends who would feel betrayed if they preached against same-sex marriage. Silence was the rule on that topic. If it was revealed to the parishioners that a priest or pastor was a homosexual, it would cause an immense scandal and demoralize and dishearten the entire parish. Beyond that, if it was a bishop, then the Diocese would be completely disrupted. I am not a homosexual, but I know some of my fellow bishops are and I do whatever I can to protect them."

"What you're saying is abortion and same-sex marriage are topics that are considered to be off limits. If either you or your fellow priests were to preach against those evils, you could be criticized or discovered for being homosexual. During your many years as a priest, did you spend any time contemplating what God's will was regarding all of this?"

"Yes, and it was always obvious to me that God would want us to give counseling and comfort to the poor sinners who found themselves suffering from these evils."

"Did God want you to warn the flock, for which you were pastor, that those sins could destroy their lives and cause them to risk losing their souls?"

"I really didn't want to rock the boat. Concentrating on charity and mercy and love of neighbor kept the peace. Besides we had bills to pay every month and collections always remained constant when no scandals were occurring."

"I'll give you something to think about as you walk to the final Checkpoint."

"God's will has always been for you to preach the truth. Jesus was obedient to His Father's will and always preached the truth, even to the point of being crucified. You and some of your priests were not even willing to be criticized for preaching the truth."

"I suppose I could have tried to do a better job"

"I will raise the gate for you bishop. The last Checkpoint is one mile down the road."

33
Apprehensive

Susan knew she was getting close to something, but just exactly what remained a mystery. Walking slowly to the final Checkpoint offered her a little more time to do a lot of thinking.

"I don't believe God exists, and I don't believe Heaven exists, but I do believe that my conscience is bothering me, and I do believe I'm approaching the end of the road. So, do I follow the advice of the angel and believe in God whom I have never seen, and then trust Him to forgive me for my sins, restore my soul and heal my conscience so I can finally have some peace? That's a lot to accomplish in a few minutes and I don't know if I have any options. I'll just have to wait till I get to the Checkpoint and see what the angel has to say."

Already populating Susan's life on his computer screen, the angel was preparing for what his experience told him would be a challenging interview. As Susan approached, he prepared to greet her.

"Good afternoon Susan, welcome to Checkpoint Three. I have reviewed your interview with the angel at Checkpoint Two and it seems you have some doubts as to how to proceed at this point."

"I do; major doubts. But I also don't know my options. Suppose I don't accept that God exists and therefore don't repent of my sins to Him. And what if I don't accept that Heaven exists either?

"Understandable questions, Susan. You are an atheist and I have the answers for you. If you don't accept that God exists and that He is your Father and Creator,then you will go to the waiting room for whatever time it takes for you to believe that He exists. Once you believe that He exists, you will begin to know Him and grow to love Him. Then, you will develop a desire to ask for His forgiveness of your sins."

"If all of that were to occur, then what would happen to me?"

"You would remain in the waiting room long enough to forgive everyone in your life, forgive yourself, and fully accept God's love and mercy and His forgiveness of your sins. Once that happens and you are certain that there is nothing in your heart or soul that is displeasing to God, you will then be accepted into Heaven."

"As you know, I don't accept that Heaven exists; are there any other options?"

"No."

"What if I don't believe that God has forgiven me?"

"That will not happen because the longer you are in the waiting room, your love for God will grow; and the truth of His mercy and forgiveness will take hold within your heart. You will see firsthand how much He suffered for you so your sins could be forgiven. In His person as God the Son, His crucifixion was His ultimate expression of His love for you. As you begin to absorb that truth, you will rejoice in His mercy and accept His forgiveness .Then, the process of healing will begin. The waiting room is a great gift of God's love and mercy for the human race."

"How much time do I have to consider all of this?"

"You may take as long as you like Susan. The waiting room is across the street, I will open the gate for you. Have a nice day."

This was Tommy's first experience of someone not believing in God. And the fact she was on the road to Heaven confused him. He knew he would need to have a conversation with the angel before he went home. But for now, he decided to just stay where he was. The bishop would be arriving any moment.

34

Rationalization

Bishop Matthews had much to think about as he approached the final checkpoint. Would the angel be more understanding than the last angel? Did he have any legitimate reasons for his silence from the pulpit? Was he really in some sort of denial, refusing to admit, even to himself, that his behavior was inexcusable?

"Good afternoon Bishop Matthews, welcome to Checkpoint Three. I would like to go over your information with you and I will have a few questions."

"Oh yes, certainly, I am happy to cooperate with you."

"Thank you, bishop. I see from your life history that you were very dedicated to helping God's people. From your early days in the seminary, even to the point of your retirement as bishop, you constantly prayed for the spiritual welfare of your parishioners and the faithful of your diocese. As a confessor, you faithfully maintained the seal of confession as you had vowed to do. And you suffered, as did many priests, when the sins of your brother priests were broadcast on television and in newspapers. Nevertheless, you and the other priests did not divulge the sins of the laity confided to them in the sacrament of reconciliation. When counseling parishioners you treated them with mercy, understanding, and were never judgmental. You were, what one would consider, a good priest. Then, of course, there is the matter of silence from the pulpit regarding the evils that destroy lives and put souls in jeopardy of losing their eternal salvation. You discussed that with the angel at the last checkpoint. But no significant acceptance of responsibility for that silence was made by you other than saying that you could have tried to do a better job. Likewise, you have not expressed any sorrow or remorse for the damage which that silence might have caused."

"I admit I was wrong, and I am sorry I didn't preach the truth as I should have. But, there was so much misbehavior among some of the priests that I was afraid of getting the wrong people in the congregation upset and have them reveal to the public any secrets that they might have been aware of. I spent years walking on eggshells not knowing who knew what, and if it could harm the church. As time progressed, it became second nature to be silent and to go along to get along. I was not a good example to the other priests, especially the good priests who wanted to do the right thing. When it came time to retire, I breathed a sigh of relief. I do, however, want to make something clear regarding my sorrow and remorse which you say I have not expressed. During my many years as a priest, I have always expressed my sorrow to God. I would confess my sins in the sacrament of reconciliation and truly try to reform. I failed, time and again, but my efforts were real and so was my sorrow. Every time I approached the pulpit with a planned homily to preach the truth, I lost my courage and spoke only of the day's readings. I suffered much because of my weakness and at times became so depressed that I wanted to leave the priesthood. God knows my heart and He knows of my sorrow."

"While your reasons for not preaching the truth seemed somewhat plausible to you at the time; your dedication to helping the souls entrusted to your care paints a picture of a much more determined personality. A personality that would stand up for what is right and not surrender to the whims of your confreres. Are you saying that the pressure from your brother priests and your fear of irate parishioners actually caused you to become someone you really are not? Is there something else that you are not mentioning?"

The bishop stared at the angel, surprised that he had asked if there was something else that he had not mentioned. And, of course, there was, but he had hoped he would never have to discuss it. Now, he had no choice.

"Yes, there is something else, something I had long ago buried in my youthful past. It was never publically revealed during my life but now that I have died, I suppose I can freely talk about it. It was very painful for me at the time, and now, even in death, it still hurts. When I graduated from high school, I had a girlfriend whom I was in love with and wanted to marry. But we decided to wait until we finished our sophomore year in college so we could save enough money from our part-time jobs to rent an apartment. At the time, we both lived at home with our parents. While I was a freshman, she became pregnant and wanted to get an abortion. I objected, telling her that abortion was taking a human being's life and I could not agree to that. She disagreed and insisted that I go along with it or she would never marry me. I still would not agree, and she said that she would obtain an abortion anyway and definitely not marry me. As the day approached, I begged her not to go through with it. She began to cry and said she didn't want to go alone and pleaded with me to at least drive her. Because I still loved her, I drove her to the clinic and went inside with her to keep her company, hoping to change her mind. I was not successful. After the abortion, we both were devastated and gradually drifted further and further apart. I would see her once in awhile but eventually, I could not concentrate on school and decided to get a full-time job. For almost a year, I was in torment about the abortion, knowing that my child had been killed. I went to confession and after many months of counseling with a good priest I decided to apply at the seminary and explore the possibility of becoming a priest. I was accepted and was ordained eight years later. When I was assigned to my first parish, the pastor was very prolife and we agreed on the necessity of preaching the truth, especially the truth about abortion. A few months later, I had decided to give my first homily exclusively on abortion. After Mass, I went outside the church to greet the parishioners and many of them spoke positively about my homily. The last person to approach me was a woman and as I looked at her, I became speechless; it was my girlfriend who I had not seen in almost nine years. She spoke in a whisper and said that she was a parishioner and if I ever spoke about abortion again, she would tell everyone at that church that I drove her to the abortion clinic and that it was my child. I knew I had a choice, tell my pastor about my past and try to be transferred to another parish, or be silent and not preach about abortion. I was too embarrassed to tell my pastor and so I opted for silence. Once I began to preach the easy homilies, and not have to put up with the complaints, I became used to the peace. Many of my brother priests behaved in the same way for one reason or another. As time progressed at that parish and subsequent parishes to which I had been assigned, I became known by my brother priests as "one of us". That was a designation I was never proud of. I knew I was not serving God as I promised Him I would. If my girl-friend had not been a member of that parish, my life as a priest would probably have been entirely different. And although my lack of courage certainly shares the responsibility for my silence from the pulpit, I nevertheless blame my girl-friend for most of it. And to this day, I still have very bitter and resentful feelings toward her. For many years, I have prayed and begged God to deliver me from my resentment towards her. But I still can't shake the anger and pain the abortion caused me and her interfering in my priesthood. I know that I have forgiven her, but every time I am confronted with the memory of this nightmare in my life, my anger and resentment return. I long to be free from all of this and I hope that in death there is some provision to help me accomplish that."

"Bishop, God is merciful as you well know. And He always welcomes the repentant sinner. Across the street is the waiting room. You can spend as much time in prayer with God as you like. He will help you with your difficulties. I will open the gate for you. Have a nice day."

Tommy had much to think about. He assumed that surely the bishop would have been admitted into Heaven. But, as he has been learning, every person's relationship with God is unique. And how everyone uses their free will during the course of their life is a determining factor in the disposition of their soul at the end of their life. While God's grace is always available to help a soul make the right decisions, a person must be receptive to God's grace. Tommy approached the angel's desk.

"Excuse me. Before I leave, I have a question about Susan."

"Sure, go ahead Tommy."

"If she didn't believe in God, and didn't believe in Heaven either, why would God allow her into Heaven?

"God created Susan, Tommy, and He loves her just as much as He loves you and me. While she says she doesn't believe in God, He knows the truth. He deposited the truth in her heart the moment He created her. Susan has been painfully wounded during the course of her life and her defense has been to reject the truth and step back somewhat from society. But deep in her heart and soul she hurts, and the moment she turns her free will in God's direction He will rescue her from her rejection of the truth. Then she will gradually begin to heal and accept God's love and mercy. Happiness and joy will finally begin to grow in her heart and eventually she will join God in Heaven."

35

Never Alone

Andy had just celebrated his sixth birthday with his Mom, Dad, and two sisters at their vacation cabin on the lake. Going for a canoe ride with his dad every year was a regular part of their summer vacation. It was Dad who had taught him how to swim when he was four years old. But this year was different. Mom had decided she would like to give it a try even though she was afraid of the water and had never learned to swim.

"Don't worry Mom, I know how to swim, and I'll save you if the canoe sinks."

"Thank you, son, but just to be sure we better bring the life jackets"

Andy ran to the shed and returned with the two orange jackets and threw them in the canoe. With the help of his Mom, he pushed the canoe into the water and off they went. The plan was to paddle along the shore of the lake and explore the areas they had not seen before. Andy and his dad had usually gone out into the middle of the lake and sometimes they would actually cross to the other side which was about a mile and a half at the widest point. After traveling along the shore for about twenty minutes, they decided to turn around and head back towards home. Andy wanted his mom to see what the shore looked like from a distance, so, they paddled about a half mile toward the center of the lake as they continued in the direction of their cabin. By the shore, the water was very calm because of an offshore breeze. But the farther out into the lake they paddled, the wind became stronger and the calm water became quite choppy.

"Andy, I think we should start paddling back towards shore, it looks like rain by our cabin and the wind is picking up."

Within five minutes, the wind picked up considerably and their paddling didn't seem to be getting them any closer to shore. Andy was in the front of the canoe and his mom was in the back. As the wind increased, it started to rain and Andy could not keep the front of the canoe pointed towards shore."

"Mom, you're stronger than I and I think we should change positions so you can keep us aiming towards shore."

As they began to change positions, the canoe turned broadside to the wind and was pushed further from shore. When they both reached the middle of the canoe, the waves tipped the canoe over and they both landed in the water. When Andy surfaced, he saw his mom struggling to swim and the canoe being pushed further away by the wind. As he swam toward her, he looked for the life jackets, but they were still in the canoe. When he reached his mom, he tried to keep her head above water but she kept going under. Desperate, he looked toward the cabin and screamed, "Dad-help us". His mom went under again and he held on to her trying to get her back to the surface. Finally, he was unable to hold his breath any longer and he had to let her go. When he reached the surface, he was too exhausted to swim and tried to float. He kicked his shoes off to make it easier to float but breathing was difficult because he had ingested so much water. He looked toward shore but could not see his dad. There was only one canoe anyway, so, unless his dad swam to him with another life jacket, Andy realized he would probably drown. An hour passed and the water was too cold to remain in for any extended period of time. Andy was growing weaker and had moments of partial consciousness. He knew it would not be long before he drowned. What he didn't know was that his dad had seen the canoe floating by itself on the opposite shore through his telescope. And because he didn't see Andy and Mom, he called the police. The police dispatched a patrol boat but that was at least 30 minutes away at the far end of the lake. Andy continued to float but would constantly have moments of unconsciousness that were becoming more frequent. Eventually, after about a half hour, he lost consciousness and rolled over face down in the water. At that very moment, a police boat was racing toward him, guided by his dad on a cell phone who had Andy in his telescope. Two minutes after Andy stopped breathing, a police officer pulled him out of the water and administered CPR and oxygen. A helicopter arrived and air lifted him to the county hospital in critical condition. For the next three weeks, the medical team struggled to keep him alive, but eventually they lost the battle and Andy died.

Tommy had finally caught up with the traffic to Heaven and was waiting at Checkpoint One for the next arrival.

"Good afternoon and welcome to Checkpoint One.
May I have your name?"

"My name is Andy. Have you seen my Mom? I tried to save her but she drowned."

"Andy, you can ask about your Mom at the next two Checkpoints, all we need to do here is go over a few questions."

"Ok".

"Do you say your prayers at night?"

"Yes, but sometimes I forget."

"Are you generous with your sisters?"

"Yes, even though they take my toys without asking."

"Are you obedient to your parents?"

"Sometimes I don't clean up my room when they tell me to. But then I get in trouble and then I clean it up."

"That's all the questions I have for you Andy, you can go on to Checkpoint Two now."

"I'm afraid to go by myself; can you just get my Mom for me?"

"I can't get your Mom for you Andy but I can request an escort."

"Well, I don't want an escort, I want my Mom. It was my fault she drowned; I should not have gone out into the middle of the lake."

Andy had tears welling up in his eyes as he began to wonder if he would ever see his Mom again.

"Please, just get my Mom for me."

The angel called her supervisor and reassured Andy that everything would be ok in a few minutes. As Andy's crying became more profound, a bright light suddenly appeared next to him. Slightly taller than Andy, the light began to fade and a young boy became visible. Andy was surprised and asked the boy his age and if he had seen his Mom. The boy replied that he was ten years old and that he would take Andy to Checkpoint Two where he could inquire about his Mom.

"Ok Andy, you will be safe now" the angel assured, "I will raise the gate and you can proceed to Checkpoint Two."

36

Faithful

Christine waited for Andy to be out of sight before she approached the Checkpoint. She had always been a considerate person and never wanted to interfere with anyone's privacy. Gradually, Andy and his escort disappeared around the first turn in the road and Christine walked to the angel's desk.

"Good afternoon and welcome to Checkpoint One. May I have your name?"

"Yes, my name is Christine."

"And what is your age, Christine?"

"I am seventy-two."

"Were you a loving person during the course of your life?"

"Yes, I always tried to be. Sometimes I held resentments toward my husband but that never lasted long, I always forgave him."

"Have you been a humble person?"

"Maybe, I hope so. It was very difficult for thirty-four years when my husband left me. I had to be very assertive and support our three children

146

financially. He never sent me any money, so I had to go to work and be the head of the family. I tried to be a good example to our children, and I was proud of the job I did. I hope that doesn't mean I wasn't humble."

"Did you ever try to convince your husband to return home?"

"Many times during the first five years, but then I gave up because he refused to leave his girlfriend with whom he was living."

"Did you pray for him in the hope that he would have a change of heart?"

"I never stopped praying for him. It was very sad for our children. They always wanted to know where daddy was. Birthdays, Christmases, graduations, it was very difficult for them. And I too was very lonely for him; I loved him and needed him in my life. He was the person I married, to share my life with, to laugh with, and to have dinner with. When we were married, we both vowed, 'until death do you part.' Because of that vow I could never leave him by marrying someone else. Then he would have no one to come home to if he ever changed his mind. God never divorces us, He is patient, always waiting for us to return."

Christine became emotional and found it difficult to continue as she cleared the tears from her eyes. The angel patiently waited, sensing that Christine wanted to continue but just needed a few minutes to compose herself.

"He left me when he was thirty. Our children were two, five, and seven. The younger ones were girls and the oldest was our son. It was very difficult for him. He really needed his dad, but his dad was never there for him. My husband said he left me because he didn't love me anymore. He never said why he didn't love me, but I knew the answer. He had met another woman and decided she was more interesting than I. As the years passed, the children finished school and eventually, they all married. I always hoped that one day he would return, especially if we had any grandchildren. Well, after our fifth grandchild was born, I received a phone call one day, and it was my husband. I was almost speechless and just listened to him as he told me that his girlfriend had left him and that he now realized what it was like to be abandoned. He asked if I would be interested in meeting with him and discussing the possibility of getting back together. I agreed to meet with him so we could discuss the situation. By that time, I was living alone. He was now sixty-four and I was sixty-two. That was ten years ago. After a very lengthy discussion, I agreed to take him back. He was very remorseful for what he had done and said that he would like to start going to church again. The last time he had been inside a church was when he lived home with me. That was thirty-four years of absence. My friends tried to convince me to not take him back. And I knew that the world had become very divorce minded and that many marriages ended in divorce. But we never were divorced and even if we had been, I would still have taken him back. Where would the human race be if God never took us back when we sin? God is merciful and forgiving and He tells us to be the same way. So, I took my husband back and for a few years our children had their father again. And our grandchildren had their grandfather. But after less than three years my husband died. He was not well and had not lived a healthy life. Now, I have died, and I hope I will see him in Heaven, if I make it to Heaven."

"You will have two more Checkpoints before you get to the end of the road Christine. I will pray that you will see your husband again. I will raise the gate for you. The next Checkpoint is one mile down the road. Have a nice day."

Tommy began to think intensely about his mom and dad. He had never considered what life would be like without them. He prayed a prayer of thanksgiving to God that his mother and father had never left him. Then he offered a prayer for Christine and her husband in the hope that they would be reunited in Heaven. Not wanting to miss Andy and his escort's arrival at Checkpoint Two, Tommy jumped on his bicycle and raced to catch them.

37
Endurance

Larry had made his last goodbyes to his many friends and was now approaching Checkpoint One. Unlike most humans, his last goodbyes were made to animals. Although he had many human acquaintances, he never really had any human friends with the exception of his mother and father. But they had passed away thirty years ago, and Larry was an only child.

"Good afternoon and welcome to Checkpoint One. May I have your name?"

"Yes, my name is Larry."

"And what is your age, Larry?"

"I am eighty-three."

"Would you say you were a loving person?"

"Yes, I always tried to be"

"Were you always forgiving to others?"

"Well, I never really had anything to forgive anyone. I mean, no one ever offended me. I didn't have too much contact with humans other than the owners of the animals I took care of. I did have to go shopping once in a while and once a year to my doctor and dentist but other than that I kind of just associated with my animals."

"What did you do for a living Larry?"

I'm a veterinarian for mostly farm animals. Sometimes the customers bring them to me and sometimes I visit the farm for the larger animals. I have a small farm myself with a few animals, plus I grow broccoli, oats, and squash. Most of it I grow for myself but the excess I sell."

"Did you attend church Larry?"

"Actually no, my parents never took me to church. But when I became an adult and got my own place to live, I went to a local church a few times but pretty much no one ever talked to me. I tried to make a few friends from time to time but people kind of avoided me."

"Why did they avoid you, Larry?"

"They never said why but I really knew the reason. It was the same reason that caused the kids in school to avoid me. In fact, they used to make fun of me all the time."

"What is the reason, Larry?"

"I'm very ugly. Can't you tell?"

"I don't see human beauty or ugliness as being something physical. I only see spiritual beauty or ugliness. I see you standing in front of me as a soul. I don't make any judgment whatsoever of your physical appearance, I concentrate only on your spiritual appearance."

"What does my spiritual appearance look like?"

"I am not permitted to discuss that with you, Larry. But I do have one more question before you move on to Checkpoint Two. Were you a humble person?"

"Well now, you got me on that one. I'm not sure how to judge if I was humble or not. If it means I was the opposite of proud, well then, I guess you could say I was humble. I mean, I was always pleased with the job I did. I always charged fair prices and did a professional job for my customers. But I never was all puffed up and high and mighty. I was just kind of regular. Do you know what I mean?"

"I do Larry, it sounds as though you were not proud, but you were humble."

"When I get to Heaven will there be any animals there? I don't want to be alone. People never wanted to be around me."

"Everyone in Heaven is different than they were on Earth, Larry. They will all be very happy to see you and they will all love you and socialize with you. Don't worry. I will now raise the gate for you, Larry. Have a nice day."

38

True Friend

Andy walked quickly with his escort to Checkpoint Two. The trauma of trying to save his mother from drowning three weeks earlier was fresh in his mind. The reality of losing his own life didn't seem to cause him much concern, but the guilt of causing his mother's death weighed heavily on his young conscience.

"I feel so badly that Mom died. It was my fault. I never should have suggested we go out further into the lake. She couldn't swim and we never put our life jackets on. My dad told me to always wear my life jacket. If the canoe had tipped over closer to shore, the wind would probably not have pushed it away and I could have reached the life jackets and Mom would still be alive."

Andy's escort remained by his side and silently listened to his concerns.

"Do you live in Heaven?"

"Yes, I do Andy."

"Do I have to wait until we get to the Checkpoint to find out about my mom or can you tell me about her?"

"Information about who is or is not in Heaven is usually not available to people who are not in Heaven."

"But you told me I could inquire about my mom when we reached the checkpoint."

"Yes, I did, and you will have to wait and see what the angel has to say."

Andy and his escort continued walking the last quarter of a mile while his escort answered many of his questions along the way.

"Good afternoon and welcome to Checkpoint Two. I see from your information that you are concerned about your mom, Andy. How may I help you?"

"I want to know if my mom is in Heaven and if you can go and get her for me. I feel really bad that she died and … Andy lost his voice and started to cry … I just want you to get my mom; please, just get my mom."

"Andy, can you answer a few questions for me?"

Trying to compose himself Andy whispered, "yes."

"Andy, would you like to tell God you are sorry for not obeying your father's instructions for wearing your life jacket? And would you like tell Him you are sorry for anything else you might have done in your life that was wrong?"

"Yes. I didn't have a chance to pray to God since I died. In the Hospital, I was always unconscious. So, I will say a prayer now. Dear God, please forgive me for being disobedient and not staying close to shore like my dad told me to. And also, please forgive me for not wearing my life jacket and not reminding my mom to wear hers. I am sorry I caused her and me to die. Amen. Was that ok? Can I see my Mom now?"

The angel was silent as the gate rose by itself. Andy's escort motioned for Andy to begin walking toward Checkpoint Three as the road ahead became illuminated.

"Are we going to see my mom now?"

The young escort smiled as he and Andy continued on the road to Heaven.

39

Imitating Jesus

Tommy remained at Checkpoint Two after Andy left with his escort. He knew that Christine would be arriving at any moment, and he was very interested in her life story. Her kindness toward her husband, who had abandoned her for all those years, impressed him. He remembered the Bible stories he had heard in church with his mom and dad and how Jesus was always forgiving people.

"I guess she must have gone to church a lot because she really imitates Jesus. I hope she gets into Heaven."

Tommy started to pray for Christine and before he finished, he noticed her walking around the last turn and proceeding to the Checkpoint.

"Welcome to Checkpoint Two, Christine. I have two questions for you. Have you forgiven everyone who offended you in your lifetime?"

"Yes, I have, and there were very few offenses I had to forgive. I always tried to see the reason for another person's anger or upset. I never regarded anyone as a bad person. I just thought of them as a good person who was weak and acted in a bad way at times."

"Here is the last question for you, Christine. Even though you remember all the sins of your life, do you completely accept God's mercy for you and His forgiveness of all your sins?"

"Yes, I do. And I had to pray about that many times. It is very difficult to ignore the memory of my life, especially those moments when I betrayed God in my moments of weakness. Jesus suffered so much to bring about our redemption and some of that suffering was certainly caused by me. And I learned after many years, that it saddens Jesus when we hold onto our guilt instead of releasing it to Him and accepting his complete forgiveness. But, I have done that now and I see that it is humility of heart and soul that brings us to that moment of accepting God's mercy and forgiveness. And so, in imitation of Jesus, I forgive everyone who has offended me in any way."

"I will raise the gate for you now Christine and you may proceed on the road to Heaven."

40

Love and Mercy

Tommy raced past Andy and his escort so he would be at Checkpoint Three when they arrived. He didn't want to miss anything. He was especially curious to find out why the road was illuminated. In the past when someone was admitted to Heaven, the area was illuminated for a brief period of time but when the soul passed into Heaven the illumination would fade and the scene would return to normal. Now the entire road from Checkpoint Two all the way to Checkpoint Three seemed illuminated. As he moved near the angel's desk, he noticed the gate was up and the illumination was gradually increasing. Moments later he could see Andy and his escort slowly rounding the turn.

"How long have you lived in Heaven?"

"For many years, Andy."

"By the way, what is your name, I never asked you your name?"

"My name is Jesus."

"Oh wow. We have someone named Jesus in our church too, only our Jesus is God. Are we going to see my mom now?"

"Yes, my mom is going to bring her to you."

Tommy began to smile as the road became even more illuminated as they approached the gate. The angel kneeled at his desk and bowed his head. Tommy did likewise. Suddenly the end of the road became extremely bright as a beautiful lady appeared with Andy's mom and moved toward him.

"Mom,'' Andy yelled as he raced to her arms. "I'm so sorry I caused you to drown."

"I love you son; don't worry, I forgive you. Thank Jesus for bringing you to me. "

Andy turned to thank Jesus, who was no longer a small boy, but was the same Jesus that Andy had in his church. They smiled at each other and in a blinding flash of light, Jesus and Mary and Andy and his mom ascended into Heaven. Tommy stared in awe as the sky slowly closed and the clouds reappeared. Turning to the angel he was surprised to see that he was still kneeling with his head bowed in prayer. He decided to wait for another opportunity to ask questions. This was a moment that deserved peace.

41

Silent Suffering

Larry approached the gate with his typical smile and peaceful demeanor. He never really had a negative outlook on life. Most of his days were spent with his animals and they never gave him a difficult time. Now, as he was traveling toward his new life, he was hopeful that many animals would be in Heaven. Especially those he had been friendly with, but who had passed away in prior years.

"Good morning, Larry, and welcome to Checkpoint Two. I see that you are wondering if animals are in Heaven."

"Yes I am. I spent most of my life with animals and it was very interesting to see how similar they are to humans. I remember, when I was a young boy, my dog was always more friendly than my classmates. They would always make me sad by making fun of me because I am so ugly. But when I arrived home, my dog would always cheer me up by running to meet me and being my friend. When I became a veterinarian, I could see all of the human characteristics evident in the behavior of animals. Many of the animals exhibited sadness when another animal was injured. I also observed animals fighting but still living together in a friendly way after that. That meant to me that they probably forgive one another. In my life, the only love I ever received from humans was when I lived with my parents. But I always received love from my dog. And since then, I have experienced love and affection from many animals. Once you gain their trust, they become very friendly and will actually seek you out during the day. They really filled the void for me most of my life. It is really natural for a human to want to give love and to be loved. But other than when I was a youngster living at home, I never really had an opportunity to express my love for anyone because they always shied away from me. As a result, I never received any love. It was a cause of great loneliness for me. As time went by, I became accustomed to friendship with the animals and I was able to give and receive love."

"Did you pray to God about this?"

"Yes, I did. And although I never expected to hear an audible answer, I knew that God answers us in many different ways. I heard that in a sermon at Church when I attended a few times many years ago. And I really came to believe that God knew very well my circumstances and probably inspired me to become a veterinarian. That way I would have animals to be friends with and I wouldn't be alone. So, as lonely as things got sometimes, I always had my animal friends. That way I could give love and receive love and be peaceful in my heart."

"Larry, I can't address your question about animals being in Heaven, but I do want to assure you that Heaven will be for you what you were hoping for all of your life. God is love, and you will be in His presence. And the people you will meet in Heaven will be filled with God's love and will joyfully share His love with you. You have one more Checkpoint before you reach Heaven, Larry. I will raise the gate for you. Have a nice day."

42

Just Reward

Tommy had remained at Checkpoint Three patiently waiting for Christine to arrive. He knew he was probably missing new arrivals at the first two Checkpoints but Andy and Christine were too interesting to ignore. Just as he was about to discuss with the angel the questions he had concerning Andy, the sky began to glow as if Jesus was approaching. Immediately, beautiful music began to play as a multitude of magnificent voices could be heard singing hymns of praise and glory to God. Suddenly, hundreds upon hundreds of souls could be seen racing heavenward in the sky as the angel began to kneel. Tommy put his bike down and knelt next to the angel. As the music began to fade, and the light began to dim, Tommy whispered to the angel "What is happening?"

"Today many souls are departing the waiting room and being united with God in Heaven. The beautiful singing voices you hear are the angels in Heaven rejoicing and praising God as His children return home to Him."

As they were conversing, Christine could be seen walking around the last turn and proceeding toward the gate. The music had stopped completely but the heavenly glow continued in the distance. The angel stood, then sat at his desk while Tommy picked up his bicycle and remained by the gate.

"Hello, Christine, and welcome to Checkpoint Three. I see that you have answered all of the questions at the first two checkpoints. And now you are at the last checkpoint and I do not have any questions for you. Do you have any questions for me?"

"Actually, I do have a question, but I don't know if it is something that I should be asking."

"You may ask anything you wish, Christine. I am sure, judging by your life, that you will not ask any question that is improper."

"Well, ok, I will ask, but if you are not allowed to answer, just tell me and I won't ask any more questions."

"Ok."

"Is my husband in Heaven?"

"I am not permitted to answer that question Christine, but I am aware of your faithfulness and devotion to your husband. What I can tell you is that souls who are treated with love and kindness during their lifetime usually respond by treating others in the same way. Your example of love and patient faithfulness to your husband most likely had a positive influence on his treatment of other people. The souls that live in Heaven are humble, loving, merciful and forgiving."

"I understand. God knows how much I prayed for my husband, and I have asked Him to save his soul. I trust God to do the best thing for my husband."

"Are you ready to go to Heaven now Christine?"

"If it is God's will, then yes I am ready."

The angel knelt down next to his desk and Tommy followed suit. The illumination of the gate to Heaven resumed and Christine was filled with magnificent joy as she smiled with the same smile she had on the day she married her husband. Suddenly she raised her hands toward Heaven as a blinding light surrounded and consumed her. Immediately, a beautiful angel carried her heavenward as the sky opened up, revealing a multitude of souls singing glorious praises to God. In seconds, the light began to dim, and the sky closed with the sound of singing slowly fading. Tommy looked at the angel who was returning to his desk and stood next to his bicycle, waiting for the right moment to ask many questions.

43

New Life

Larry approached the final checkpoint with anxious anticipation. He trusted God and knew that He was faithful and would reward those who had been faithful to Him. He hoped that he would see his parents and his animal friends, but he didn't know if he would still be ugly. If he looked the same and he met some of his fellow students from his school days, would they be nice and loving as the angel had said? Or would they be friendly and then as soon as he was out of sight start laughing and making fun of him as they usually did?

"Good morning Larry and welcome to Checkpoint Three."

"Good morning. I was told that this is the last Checkpoint before entering Heaven?"

"Yes, it is Larry. And I have a question for you."

"Ok."

"What is your greatest hoped for reality when you enter Heaven?"

"I hope to finally be loved by humans. And I fear that if I continue to look like I do now that will never happen."

"The angel at Checkpoint Two has already assured you that you will be loved by everyone in Heaven. Do you not believe him?"

"I believe him, but I lived so long without human love that it is difficult to imagine. I remember driving past a church one day and it had one of those signs outside which displayed messages. It had a quotation from Saint Mother Teresa that said, 'The greatest suffering is to be unwanted, unneeded and unloved.' And that was what my life was like. Yes, I did have the love from the animals. But I never heard the words 'I love you' from a human being after my parents died. That was forty years of feeling 'unwanted, unneeded and unloved.'"

"When I asked you what your greatest hoped for reality would be upon entering Heaven, I was trying to help you see the purpose of Heaven. Naturally you will want to be with family and friends, and in your case the animals too, but the main purpose of Heaven is to be with God. He is your happiness and joy. He gave you your family and friends and all the animals. And when you are reunited with Him, He will be very happy and joyful too. He created you in His image and likeness and His likeness is love. God is love. His essence is giving and receiving love and He has shared that with you and everyone else. The people in Heaven have given and received love as God has inspired them to do. That is why they were happy on earth and now are happy in Heaven with Him."

"Gee, I guess because I never spent much time in church, I never heard the truth as you have just described it. People probably shared what they learned in church with one another, and everyone become informed. Unfortunately, I never had anyone share any of this with me because humans always avoided me. But the animals never avoided me and they loved me and I loved them. Because God is love I imagine that that was pleasing to Him. He knew that I didn't have any human friends."

"Yes, your behavior was pleasing to God, and I wanted you to have this knowledge of God and His love for you before you meet Him."

"When will I meet Him?"

"He is coming for you now."

The light of Heaven instantly shown down upon Larry as the angel knelt and Larry gazed at the sky. There he could see Jesus and the angels approaching him as he was raised into Heaven with a look of magnificent joy on his face. He put his hands to his face and realized it was a face that no one had ever seen before. It was a new face, a face of Heavenly beauty which God had given him. Larry was safe now and would rejoice in God's presence forever. His sadness had been turned into joy.

44

Class Dismissed

Tommy was anxious to ask the angel many questions after Christine went to Heaven, but before he could begin Larry had approached the gate. Now with Larry in Heaven and what seemed like a pause in new arrivals Tommy walked to the angel's desk.

"So much has happened recently. Is it ok to ask you some questions now?"

"Tommy, many of the questions you have will be answered by the angel who is going to escort you back to town. The angel will know your questions before you ask them, so just let him speak and I'm sure you will have all the answers you need."

"Escort me back to town; what do you mean?"

"Tommy, you were given the privilege of seeing and hearing the many types of circumstances that souls encounter on their way to Heaven. While they all had eventually led lives that put them on the road to Heaven, they had not yet reached that point where they would be admitted to Heaven or sent to the waiting room. They still had time to make decisions which would reveal the true nature of their hearts. If they were loving, kindhearted, charitable, humble, and forgiving, they went to Heaven. But if they were selfish, proud, resentful, mean-spirited or vengeful, then they went to the waiting room. And while they were described as being dead, they were still in the last moments of their life. Their souls' had not yet left their bodies and they still had free will. The young man Billy, who returned to earth, was given another chance at life. He, like all the others, was not completely dead. The three Checkpoints represent the patience of God. He gives everyone endless chances during their lives to change course and turn back to Him. He desires that no one be lost and that all be saved for eternal life. His love and mercy are everlasting. But everyone must have a change of heart, repent of their sinfulness, ask God to forgive them, accept His forgiveness and love, and accept Him. Now, when you return to earth, you will have many lessons to share with your family and friends."

"Will I be allowed back again?"

"No. The next time I will see you is when you die."

"When will that be?"

"I don't know."

"Well, thank you for all of your answers. When will the angel be escorting me back?"

"Right now, he is standing behind you."

"Good morning Tommy. Just hold onto my arm and I'll give you a ride to the entrance."

"In five seconds Tommy covered the three miles he had traveled many times before while pedaling his bicycle."

"Wow that was really fast. But I just realized we left my bike back at the Checkpoint."

"No, we didn't Tommy. There it is leaning against the oak tree right where it was when you started your journey."

"I had a lot of questions, but it seems the answers are already in my memory. How did that happen?"

"I put them there for you. But you still have one more question. I didn't answer that one for you just in case you would like to change your mind and not ask it."

"Oh, uh yes, I do have one more question. It is a serious question. But even though the answer could be scary I will ask it anyway. This is the road to Heaven. Where is the road to Hell?"

"Follow me."

The angel walked past the entrance and stood at the edge of the road and pointed into town as the cars drove by.

"This is the road to Hell. It leads into town, and then into cities, and all the vanities and evils the world has to offer. These are the things that draw souls away from God and enslave them in a life of selfishness and sin. God in His great love and mercy gives them chance after chance to turn away from sin and turn back to Him. The souls you encountered did return to God during their lives, some more than others. All of them will eventually be in Heaven. But those who travel on the road to Hell are living very dangerous lives and they never know when the moment of death will come. Unless they repent and return to God, they could lose their souls. And that would mean going to Hell. So, while you live Tommy, do all you can to help God save the souls of His children. He loves every one of them and will be very grateful for your help."

"I will do my best."

"It's time for me to leave you now. So, continue on your way home from school. God Bless you Tommy."

As the angel disappeared Tommy moved his bicycle away from the road to Heaven and began to pedal towards home once again. As he slowly moved past the stores and shops, he noticed a building he had passed many times before but never took the time to read the sign out front. "Faith & Hope Family Counseling Center" was directly on the corner of a busy side street. As he waited for the traffic to pass, so he could safely cross, he noticed a young man walking down the sidewalk and suddenly enter the building.

"Gee, he looks familiar. Where have I seen him before?"

Because it was springtime the front windows were open, and Tommy could hear the phones ringing and people talking.

"Good afternoon, Faith and Hope Family Counseling, how may I direct your call? Yes, she is, one moment please. Stephanie, you have a call on line Two.

"Welcome Billy, I have some paperwork for you to fill out. Please have a seat, Stephanie is on the phone and will be with you shortly."

"Wow; that is the same Billy who was on the road to Heaven. I knew I recognized him. My mom will never believe any of this."

When Tommy prayed for God to give him a special way in which to serve, he could not have asked for or imagined a more perfect gift. As he began to pedal home, he reflected on the day he would remember for all eternity.

Helpful Prayers

We spend a great deal of time – most of our life – living for ourselves and for whatever we consider important. But we spend precious little time preparing for the life to come. How much sense does *that* make? After all, eternity is a long time to spend being dissatisfied.

Never let anything so distress you that you forget the joy of the resurrection.   *St. Mother Teresa*

You cannot do a kindness too soon because you never know how soon it will be too late.
                    Ralph Waldo Emerson

Think of your life as a river. Are you flowing toward God or away from Him?

Conscience has been described as the gentle pressure of God's hand on our hearts.

It is said that a dog is a man's best friend. But, who created the dog?

Let nothing disturb you, nothing cause you fear. All things pass; God is unchanging. Patience obtains all: Whoever has God needs nothing else. God alone suffices.   *St. Teresa of Avila*

Faith has been described as "A profound, deep, and intimate relationship with God".

The everlasting God has in His wisdom foreseen from eternity the cross that He now presents to you as a gift from His inmost heart. This cross He now sends you, He has considered with His all-knowing eyes, understood with His divine mind, tested with His wise justice, warmed with loving arms and weighed with His own hands to see that it be not one inch to large and not one ounce too heavy for you. He has blessed it with His holy name, anointed it with His grace, perfumed it with His consolation, taken one last glance at you and your courage, and then sent it to you from Heaven, a special greeting from God to you, alms of the all-merciful love of God.   *St. Francis de Sales*

Prayer opens the door of your heart to God. And once you invite Him in, your life will never be the same.

T

Prayer before the Cross

Jesus by this saving sign, bless this listless soul of mine. Jesus by your feet nailed fast, mend the missteps of my past. Jesus with your riven hands, bend my will to loves demands. Jesus, in your heart laid bare, warm my inner coldness there. Jesus by your thorn crowned head, still my pride till it is dead. Jesus by your muted tongue, stay my words that hurt someone. Jesus by your tired eyes, open mine to faith's surprise. Jesus by your fading breath, keep me faithful until death. Yes, Lord, by this saving sign, save this wayward soul of mine.

God has created me to do some definite service; God has committed some work to me which has not been committed to another. I have my mission – I may never know it in this life, but I shall be told in the next. I am a link in a chain, a bond of connection between persons. God has not created me for nothing. I shall do good; I shall do God's work. I shall be an angel of peace, a preacher of truth in my own place while not intending it if I do but keep God's commandments. Therefore, I will trust God – whatever, wherever I am. I can never be thrown away. If I am in sickness, my sickness may serve God; in perplexity, my perplexity may serve God; in sorrow, my sorrow may serve God. God does nothing in vain. God knows what He is about. God may take away my friends; God may throw me among strangers. God may make me feel desolate, make my spirits sink, hide my future from me – still, God knows what He is about.

St. John Henry Newman

God of Life, there are days when the burdens we carry chafe our shoulders and wear us down; when the road seems dreary and endless, the skies grey and threatening; when our lives have no music in them, and our hearts are lonely, and our souls have lost their courage. Flood the path with light, we beseech Thee; turn our eyes, to where the skies are full of promises...   *St. Augustine*

Have no fear for what tomorrow may bring. The same loving God who cares for you today will take care of you tomorrow and every day. God will either shield you from suffering or give you unfailing strength to bear it. Be at peace, then, and put aside all anxious thoughts and imaginings.

St. Francis de Sales

I am going to the home of my Father. I am frightened and alone along the way. I am not worthy to return Home. I have offended my Father deeply. I have broken all His rules and laws. I have hurt myself; I have damaged my soul. I have snuffed out the Light of God within me. I have scarred the Image of God that I was made in. I do not deserve to be welcomed back into the Home of my Father. But I see Him waiting for me now at the end of the road. He is running to me, weeping. He picks me up and holds me and tells me everything will be all right, because I am home now. I am home with my Father, my God.

I am only one, but I am one. I cannot do everything, but I can do something. And because I cannot do everything, I will not refuse to do the something that I can do. What I can do, I should do. And what I should do, by the grace of God, I will do.

Edward Everett Hale

Eye has not seen, nor ear heard, neither has it entered into the heart of man, what God has prepared for those who love Him.

1 Corinthians 2:9 NAB

It is not enough to discover Christ … you must bring Him to others! The world today is one great mission land, even in countries of long-standing Christian tradition.

St. John Paul II

Dear Jesus, in your great love and mercy, touch the hearts of expectant mothers who are planning to have abortions. Give them the grace and strength to *change* their minds, and with your loving help they will give birth to the babies destined for them.

If sometimes our poor people have had to die of starvation, it is not because God didn't care for them, but because you and I didn't give, were not instruments of love in the hands of God, to give them that bread, to give them that clothing, because we did not recognize Christ, when once more Christ came in distressing disguise.

St. Mother Teresa

What does love look like? It has the hands to help others. It has the feet to hasten to the poor and needy. It has eyes to see misery and want. It has the ears to hear the sighs and sorrows of men and women. That is what love looks like.

St. Augustine

When for love of God, we share our goods with our neighbor in need, we discover that the fullness of life comes from love and all is returned to us as a blessing in the form of peace, inner satisfaction and joy. *Pope Benedict XVI*

Hail Holy Queen, Mother of Mercy, our life, our sweetness and our hope! To you do we cry poor banished children of Eve; to you do we send up our sighs, mourning and weeping in this vale of tears. Turn, then, most gracious advocate, your eyes of mercy toward us; and after this our exile, show unto us the blessed fruit of your womb, Jesus. O clement, O loving, O sweet Virgin Mary. Pray for us, O holy Mother of God, that we may be made worthy of the promises of Christ.   Amen

St. Michael the Archangel, defend us in battle; be our protection against the wickedness and snares of the devil. May God rebuke him, we humbly pray, and do thou, O prince of the Heavenly Host, by the power of God, cast into hell, satan and the other evil spirits, who prowl through the world, seeking the ruin of souls.   Amen!

No one is outside of God's mercy.

I hope my children look back on today and see a mother who had time to play. There will be years for cleaning and cooking, for children grow up while we're not looking.   Author unknown.

Discover to me, Oh my God, the nothingness of this world, the greatness of Heaven, the shortness of time, and the length of eternity. Grant that I may prepare for death, escape hell, and in the end, obtain Heaven, through the merits of our Lord Jesus Christ. Amen

Stop judging and you will not be judged.
Stop condemning and you will not be condemned. Forgive and you will be forgiven. Give and gifts will be given to you; a good measure, packed together, shaken down, and overflowing, will be poured into your lap. For the measure with which you measure will in return be measured out to you.

Luke: 6:37 NAB

God loves us unconditionally with a love we cannot earn or ever be worthy of. And He loves us for ourselves, not as we should be, or possibly could be, but as we are – warts and all, with our psychological quirks and spiritual infidelities.

Fr. *Damian Towey C.P.*

The Miracle Prayer

Lord Jesus, I come before you just as I am.
I am sorry for my sins, I repent of my sins, please
forgive me. In your name, I forgive all others for
what they have done against me. I renounce satan,
the evil spirits and all their works. I give you my
entire self Lord Jesus, now and forever. I invite you
into my life Jesus. I accept you as my Lord, God and
Savior. Heal me, change me, strengthen me in
body, soul and spirit. Come Lord Jesus, cover me
with your precious blood, and fill me with your
Holy Spirit. I love you Lord Jesus. I praise you Jesus.
I trust you Jesus. I thank you Jesus. I shall follow
you every day of my life.   Amen

The fruit of the Holy Spirit is love, peace, patience,
joy, gentleness, kindness, goodness, faithfulness,
and self control.   Galatians 5:22-23 NAB

Right is right, even if no one is doing it.
Wrong is wrong even if everybody is doing it.
St. Augustine

He who plants the smallest kindness,
sows indeed a mighty seed.

Prayer of St. Gertrude the Great

"Eternal Father, I offer Thee the Most Precious Blood of Thy Divine Son, Jesus, in union with the Masses said throughout the world today, for all the holy Souls in Purgatory.   Amen."

Our Lord told St. Gertrude the Great that this prayer would release 1,000 Souls from Purgatory each time it is said.

"A new commandment I give to you,
that you love one another,
even as I have loved you,
that you also love one another."
John 13:34 NAB

In whatever you do, remember your last days, and you will never sin.   Sirach 7: 38 NAB

Blessed are the merciful, for they will be shown mercy.   Matt 5:7 NAB

Oh Holy Spirit, soul of my soul, I adore you. Enlighten, guide, strengthen and console me. Tell me what I ought to do and command me to do it. I promise to be submissive to whatever you permit to happen to me, only show me what is your will.   Amen

"Our Father who art in Heaven, hallowed be thy name. Thy kingdom come, thy will be done, on earth as it is in Heaven. Give us this day our daily bread, and forgive us our trespasses as we forgive those who trespass against us, and lead us not into temptation but deliver us from evil."   Amen

"The highest form of worship is to find the least among you and treat them like Jesus."
                    St. Mother Teresa of Calcutta

    You give but little when you give of your possessions. It is when you give of yourself that you truly give.   Khalil Gibran

Meeting God in Heaven

Last night, I had a dream that I died and went to Heaven. I was told by an angel that God was waiting to speak with me. As I slowly approached Him, many thoughts raced through my mind. I knew this meeting had been planned for a very long time. I knew what I was bringing to the meeting. So did God. I was anxious. As I moved closer, God's face slowly came into view. We didn't speak - his face overwhelmed me with love. His mercy consumed me. My soul cried bitterly for the missed opportunities to love my neighbor, which I had been guilty of, again and again and again. I tried to speak but my sadness took my breath away as I could see that He had been my neighbor. My knees grew weak as I desperately tried to apologize. Trembling, I looked into His eyes, silently pleading for His help. Quietly, He stepped forward, embraced me with His immense love and mercy, looked into my eyes, and gently said "Welcome home."

Special Act of Sorrow

Forgive my sins, O Lord, forgive me my sins; the sins of my youth, the sins of my age, the sins of my soul, the sins of my body; my idle sins, my serious voluntary sins, the sins I know, the sins I have concealed so long, and which are now hidden from my memory. I am truly sorry for every sin, mortal and venial, for all the sins of my childhood up to the present hour. I know my sins have wounded Thy tender Heart, O my Savior, let me be freed from the bonds of evil through the most bitter passion of my Redeemer. Oh my Jesus, forget and forgive what I have been.   Amen

"Come, you who are blessed by my Father. Inherit the Kingdom prepared for you from the foundation of the world."   Matt: 25: 34 NAB

"In my Father's house there are many dwelling places. If there were not, would I have told you that I am going to prepare a place for you? And if I go and prepare a place for you, I will come back again and take you to myself, so that where I am you also may be."   John 14: 2-3 NAB

"The greatest love,
 The greatest mercy,
 The greatest charity,
  is to teach another person the truth.
 The truth sets us free.
 There isn't enough truth in our world."

 Bishop Joseph E. Strickland
 Diocese of Tyler

"One must become accustomed to thinking confidently about the mystery of death, so that the definitive encounter with God occurs in a climate of interior peace, in the awareness that He "who knit me in my mother's womb" will receive us."

Saint John Paul II,   January 2005

"One thing is necessary; that the sinner set ajar the door of his heart, be it ever so little, to let in a ray of God's merciful grace, and then God will do the rest."

Saint Faustina (1507)

Eye has not seen, nor ear heard, neither has it entered into the heart of man, what God has prepared for those who love Him.

                    1 Corinthians 2:9 NAB

About the author

In his professional life, John Regan was a radio news broadcaster, television weatherman, business owner, President of Network for Re-entry Prison Ministry and President of Palm Beach County Right to Life League Inc. Now, as an author, John continues in his efforts to bring souls to Jesus for their salvation by writing...

Heaven - Who gets in and who must wait - his seventh book which follows the very popular *Return of the Children.* Married to his wife Joan for fifty-seven years, they live in South Florida with their three children, eight grandchildren, and four great grandchildren. John may be reached at:

johnregan2100@gmail.com

jreganjr@protonmail.com

561-515-9633

Your comments are welcome.

To order:

Amazon.com

or

www.heavenwhogetsin.com

or

johnregan2100@gmail.com

Other books by John:

Return of the Children
The Monk & the Skunk
Please
Little Bluey learns to fly.